P9-ELV-477

Waiting
for
You

Waiting for You

SUSANE COLASANTI

VIKING

VIKING
Published by Penguin Group
Penguin Group (USA) Inc., 345 Hudson Street, New York, New York 10014, U.S.A.
Penguin Group (Canada), 90 Eglinton Avenue East, Suite 700, Toronto, Ontario, Canada M4P 2Y3
(a division of Pearson Penguin Canada Inc.)
Penguin Books Ltd, 80 Strand, London WC2R 0RL, England
Penguin Ireland, 25 St Stephen's Green, Dublin 2, Ireland (a division of Penguin Books Ltd)
Penguin Group (Australia), 250 Camberwell Road, Camberwell, Victoria 3124, Australia
(a division of Pearson Australia Group Pty Ltd)
Penguin Books India Pvt Ltd, 11 Community Centre, Panchsheel Park, New Delhi – 110 017, India
Penguin Group (NZ), 67 Apollo Drive, Rosedale, North Shore 0632, New Zealand
(a division of Pearson New Zealand Ltd)
Penguin Books (South Africa) (Pty) Ltd, 24 Sturdee Avenue, Rosebank, Johannesburg 2196, South Africa

Penguin Books Ltd, Registered Offices: 80 Strand, London WC2R 0RL, England

First published in the U.S.A. by Viking, a member of Penguin Group (USA) Inc., 2009

7 9 10 8 6

LIBRARY OF CONGRESS CATALOGING-IN-PUBLICATION DATA
Colasanti, Susane.
Waiting for you / by Susane Colasanti.
p. cm.
Summary: Fifteen-year-old high school sophomore Marisa, who has an anxiety disorder,
decides that this is the year she will get what she wants—a boyfriend and a social life—
but things do not turn out exactly the way she expects them to.
ISBN 978-0-670-01130-8 (hardcover)
[1. Interpersonal relations—Fiction. 2. Dating (Social customs)—Fiction.
3. Anxiety disorders—Fiction. 4. High schools—Fiction. 5. Schools—Fiction.
6. Family life—Fiction. 7. Divorce—Fiction.] I. Title.
PZ7.C6699Wai 2009
[Fic]—dc22
2008046977

Printed in U.S.A.
Set in Minion
Book design by Sam Kim

For everyone out there who is still waiting

Waiting
for
You

*

August–October

*

1

The best thing about summer camp is the last day. Because that's the day you get to go home and live like a normal person again.

Don't get me wrong. Camp was freaking awesome. I spent the entire summer in Maine at a special camp for the arts. My dad gave me his old Nikon camera and taught me how to develop photos last year, and ever since then photography has been my passion. There's something about vintage film that captures the Now in a way digital can't. It just makes everything look softer somehow. And the whole old-school method of developing your own photos exactly how you want them is really cool.

So yeah, I learned a lot more about photography at camp and had a ton of practice. I've also been playing the violin since seventh grade, so I had violin lessons there, too. We even had a concert last night.

I've only been home for like three hours but I've already participated in the following critical post-camp activities:

- Took a real shower. With water pressure. That actually got me clean.

- Remembered what air-conditioning felt like. Did a little happy dance at the supermarket.

- Put on clothes that didn't smell like mildew. They also did not feel permanently damp.

- Sat on the couch and watched TV.

- Got a cold drink from the refrigerator. Ice rules.

The only thing left on my list is to get together with Sterling for the first time since June, so I'm majorly stoked. I can't wait to see her. Not just because she's my best friend, but because school starts in a week and we're getting psyched for it.

I love the beginning of the year. It's all about renewal and reinventing yourself, becoming the person you've always wanted to be. You can go back to school as a whole new person and have a totally different time. Every year I get all excited about how everything's going to be different, but it never really is. I'm tired of always being disappointed. This has to be our year.

It feels good to knock on Sterling's door with "Wheel" playing in my head. Like I've come full circle after a long journey, even though I've only been at sleep-away camp for two months. But this is such a "Wheel" moment. That song rocks. The best part is where John Mayer says how our connections are permanent, how if you drift apart from someone there's always a chance you can be part of their life again. How everything comes back around again. I have a theory that the answers to all of life's major questions can be found in a John Mayer song.

Sterling flings the door open. Her hair isn't brown anymore. Now it's blonde.

"Oh my god, your *hair*!" I yell.

Then she grabs me and we're hugging and squealing and doing this thing where we're hopping around.

"I know!" Sterling goes. "It was supposed to come out more like yours, but the stylist said your color is complicated."

"Why didn't you tell me you were dyeing it?"

"I wanted it to be a surprise."

"Oh, I'm surprised."

"So, what do you think?" Sterling twirls around so I can inspect her hair from all angles. It's a lighter blonde than mine, since my hair has different shades of blonde mixed in, and I'm not sure if it works with her coloring.

"It's hot," I say. Maybe I just have to get used to it.

She points to my usual stool in the kitchen. "Sit," she says.

Sterling took over the kitchen when she was twelve because her mom can't cook. Plus, she's never here. And Sterling got sick of eating things like hot dogs and Tater Tots and those instant pasta sides every night for dinner. So one day, Sterling announced that she was doing all of the cooking. Now she takes cooking classes and everything. Her mom was thrilled. The agreement is that

Sterling puts what she needs for the week on the grocery list and her mom gets everything.

There are four different pots going on the stove. Vegetables in all different colors compete for space on the counter. Two place mats are set out across from each other on the other counter where we always sit, with cloth napkins and schmancy silverware.

"You didn't have to do all this," I go.

"Of course I did. What kind of lame welcome home dinner did you think I was making?"

"Yeah, but it's so . . . extensive." I had to beg my parents to let me come over to Sterling's for dinner since it's my first day back and all, but they finally let me. And we're going to a pier party after.

"Only the best for you, friend girl."

"Wow." Something bubbles in one of the pots. Everything smells so good. "Thanks for doing all this."

"Please. You're the one who's doing me a favor. No one's tried any of this stuff yet. Well, except for me, but I'm not exactly impartial." Sterling picks something out of a bowl and stuffs it in her mouth. "I can't stop eating these," she says. "Try one."

I peer into a bowl of weird-shaped cracker thingies that look like someone cut them out of cardboard. "What is it?"

"Feng Shui rice crackers." Sterling used to have this tone with me when I asked her what something was, like, *How can you not know this?* But now she's used to my culinary ignorance. My family is basically the meat-and-potatoes kind.

Slowly, I stretch my hand into the bowl, as if a rice cracker might bite me. They feel kind of sticky. But I don't want to insult Sterling, so I take a small bite of my cracker. "Hmm."

"Aren't they *so* good?"

I guess I'm not a rice cracker person. "They're . . . different," I tell her. Which I know will make her happy. That's like the highest compliment you can give Sterling about anything going on in her kitchen. She's into the exotic.

"I know." She chomps into another cracker. "I've already eaten like a whole bag of these."

It's hard not to be jealous of Sterling. She's so tiny, but she eats constantly. If I even look at a doughnut I immediately gain five pounds.

Sterling darts to the stove and multitasks between two pans and a massive pot.

"What are you making?" I ask.

"Risotto. Wait, I have to concentrate on this part. It's all about the timing."

While we're eating, Sterling tells me about her new lifestyle plan. She got on the self-improvement train the first day of summer vacay and is riding it right into sophomore year. "Okay. So." She puts her fork down. "Do you need more sauce?"

"No, I'm good." Everything tastes incredible. Sterling could be a professional chef right now, and people eating at her restaurant would never know she's only fifteen. You know, if she stayed hidden in the kitchen and all.

"So," she goes. "You know how I'm kind of high-strung?"

"Pretty much."

"Guess what I'm into now?"

"Uh . . . competitive Ping-Pong?"

"No."

"Auto repair?"

"No! Guess real guesses."

"I give up."

Sterling puts her hands up, like, *Wait for it.* Then she announces: "Yoga!"

"Yoga?"

"Is that cool or what?"

I'm kind of leaning toward "or what." If it was anyone but Sterling, I'd agree that it's cool. But she's the most hyperactive person I know. Her attention span is nonexistent unless a recipe is involved. She can't even sit still for more than three minutes. And now she's doing yoga? How is that possible?

Of course, I can't say any of this. I'm her best friend. I have to be supportive.

So I go, "Is it fun?"

"It's already changing my life! I can *feel* my concentration improving."

"That's awesome."

"Totally. Now you."

We do this every year. We get together before school starts, when all of the electric energy of possibility is zinging around, and make a pact on how we want our lives to change.

"I'm tired of waiting for my real life to start," I go. "Like, when's all the good stuff finally going to happen?"

"Now! This is our year!"

"How do you know?"

"I can just tell."

I really hope she's right. There's only so much waiting a person can endure until they start thinking that maybe nothing exciting will ever happen to them. Like, *ever.*

"Your waiting is over," Sterling insists. "Trust me."

The problem with the last few days of summer? Is that you can't hold on to them. They zoom by way too fast. You live through them in a dream until they're over. And then everything slows down to a glacial pace again.

Usually I'm not nervous until the day before school starts. But today I'm already nervous because we're going to Andrea's pier party tonight and everyone will be there. Or at least the one person I'm extra nervous about seeing will be there.

When we get to Andrea's house, we go around back and find her sitting on the sand. She waves us over.

"Hey, you guys," Andrea says. "How was your summer?"

"Awesome," we both say together. I glance around for him while trying to look like I'm not looking for anyone.

And then I see him.

There's a volleyball game and Derek is serving the ball. His shirt is off and his bathing suit is sexy. It's red and has a thin neon orange stripe along the seam. It's so perfect that he plays volleyball because he's got that classic California surfer boy look. If we didn't live in Connecticut, you'd totally think he was from San Diego or something.

I watch him play. I haven't fully absorbed how perfect his body is yet.

"Hello! Earth to Marisa!"

I snap out of my Derek trance. Sterling and Andrea are looking up at me. When did Sterling spread her towel out? How long was I staring at Derek? And did everyone see me staring at him like a total loser?

Okay, remain calm. Remember: Control your thoughts to control your actions.

I spread my towel out and try to concentrate on what they're saying. As usual, Sterling's drooling over some boy who's too old for her.

"Who's that?" she asks Andrea.

"Who, Dan?" Andrea goes. "He's my brother's friend from college."

"How old is he?"

"Like, twenty-one? Twenty-two?"

"Does he have a girlfriend?" Sterling wants to know.

Andrea gives her a look.

"What?"

"Why can't you like boys your own age?"

"Ew! Maybe because they're gross?"

She has a point. But so does Andrea. Sterling always likes guys who are way out of her age range. And then she complains when all they do is flirt with her.

"I'm just saying," Andrea goes.

"Yeah, well *I'm* just saying that Dan is seriously hot," Sterling says. "Can you introduce me?"

Andrea scrunches her face up.

"What?" Sterling goes.

Andrea's all, "Forget it." But she obviously thinks Sterling's a slut for going after older guys. Sterling's never done anything with any of them, though.

Sterling's like, "Could it *be* any hotter?"

I go, "In hell, maybe."

"The water's great," Andrea says. "You guys should go in."

"Sweet. Coming?" Sterling asks me.

"I'm good."

"I'll go," Andrea says. "I'm completely crispy."

At first, I watch them in the water and talk to some girls I know from orchestra and convince myself that I shouldn't stare at Derek anymore. But that doesn't really work, because I keep sneaking looks at him.

And then something amazing happens. Something seriously life-altering.

Derek looks over at me and smiles.

He's smiling right at me!

I think I smile back, but I'm not sure if my face is working right. He does this little wave thing and goes back to the game.

I wish it could stay like this forever, with the anticipation of everything.

It's always weird seeing everyone when summer's over. There are kids who got tanner. Kids who got thinner. Kids who totally changed their hair. It's interesting to see how people reinvent themselves over the summer. I wonder if anyone thinks I've changed.

Walking home in the dark, I see Nash out on our dock. He's sitting under the lamplight, probably getting a head start on whatever we have to read for English. It's so weird that I don't really know him anymore, because he used to be such a fixture in my life. We played together in third and fourth grades. We practically lived out on the dock all summer, swimming in the river and playing water games. But then everything changed when middle school started. I just didn't feel like hanging out with him as much anymore. The thing is, I can't remember why.

We've known each other forever. Far Hills is one of those small Connecticut towns where everyone knows everyone else. Where you go to school with the same exact kids from kindergarten until you graduate. Plus, Nash and I are neighbors. He lives three houses down, and we still use the same dock for swimming in the summer (our town is on a peninsula, sticking out into Five Mile River).

We actually like using the dock all year. It's a really good place to go when you need some space. It's just that now we avoid using it if the other one's already out there. Sometimes when I see Nash on it, I want to go over and say hi or something, the way we used to do all those years ago. But then it's like he got there first so I should respect his privacy. I know what it's like when you just need to be alone for a while and block out the world.

It's strange how you can live so close to someone and grow up with him without ever really knowing who he is. Or maybe you used to know him, but now you're like strangers. It's weird how time can change something you thought would always stay the same.

2

Can I just say that when you're hoping things will get better but they don't, it majorly sucks?

I really, really thought that today would be different. I imagined getting to school and everyone reacting to me like I'm not such a freak anymore. But that's not how the first day of school is going. It's bad. Like, desperately bad. Because when everyone expects you to be a certain way, it's really hard to escape that image. It's like once everyone decides who you are, you're locked into their version of you and that's it. And everyone decided I was crazy last year. But I'm determined to break out of that. I have to believe that there might be a possible escape route for me.

Sterling seems fine. But she's always fine. She's little and cute and people like her. We don't have any classes together this year and I have no idea how I'll survive lunch. I saw her in the hall when we got our locker assignments and she was talking to people and laughing like she wasn't even nervous. I always have a knot in my stomach on the first day of school that doesn't go away until I get home. Plus, I can never fall asleep the night before, so I'm trying to handle the disaster of my life on two hours' sleep.

I was expecting people to realize that I've changed. I made an effort to smile at people and say hi in homeroom, but I was basically ignored.

Why doesn't anyone want to talk to me? I mean, other than the same people I've been talking to for years. I was sort of hoping to make some new friends. I only have a few friends and I find that to be lame. Lots of kids go out in these big groups. That would be so fun.

Whatever. I can't even deal with this now because we're supposed to be doing a getting-to-know-you activity in chemistry. I hate it when teachers make you sit in a circle on the first day of school and do some activity where you have to introduce yourself. It's like, every nerve in your body is already twanging, which is bad enough. The last thing you want to do is talk in front of people. How can teachers not know that?

So I guess it isn't too heinous that Mrs. Hunter is making us do this activity in pairs. We already got assigned seats. I sit in front of Nash. Then we got this sheet of questions and we had to pick ten that we would most want to ask a potential friend. Which isn't a bad idea if you think about it. Being able to interview your potential friends would rock. Because then you wouldn't get so many nasty surprises later. It's not like you can take back a friendship.

After we pick our ten questions, I turn my desk around to face Nash.

Nash goes first. "If you were a shape, which shape would you be and why?"

I smile at my paper. That was the weirdest question, which is why it was my favorite.

"What?" Nash goes.

"I picked the shape one, too."

"So what shape would you be?"

"Hmm."

I have to seriously think about that. Not only am I sitting in front of this boy for the rest of the year, but we're also lab partners. Which means we have to do every lab report together, plus a few big projects. So if I make a sucky impression and he thinks I'm a reject, it'll be really hard to prove him wrong after that.

Okay, so it's not the first time he's meeting me. But this is the first time we've said more than three words to each other since elementary school and I want to make a good impact on everyone today. I don't just care about how I look (shoulder-length blonde hair with natural highlights, brown eyes that have these green flecks if the light hits them the right way, not fat or skinny, white T-shirt, jeans, black Converse). It's also important to make sure my new personality is showing.

"I'd be . . . a circle," I go. "Within a square."

"I think you're only supposed to pick one."

"Well, I can't be defined by just one shape."

"I see."

"I'm a very complex person," I say, even though I'm not. But I feel daring and wild, saying it. Like I could be anybody and he wouldn't even know the difference.

"I'm getting that," Nash goes. He has this glint in his eyes and a smile where his mouth only turns up on one side.

Don't let that fool you. He's not potential boyfriend material.

Here's why. Nash is totally geeked out. His hair is always messy, his shirts usually look like he slept in them, and he constantly has to correct people when they're wrong, in this annoying know-it-ally way. His social skills are pathetic and I want more friends, so we don't exactly have the same priorities. Plus, I've seen him lick his fingers at lunch when the napkin is like *right there*.

There's just no way.

Nash does have some good qualities, though. I like how he's really shy and sweet. He's not like most other boys who are always acting all doofusy and fifth-grade about everything, where it's like, *Hello, we're in tenth grade now, grow up already.* Nash seems a lot more mature. He's the type of person Aunt Katie would say has an "old soul."

All those good things about him were enough when we were younger, catching fireflies in the summer and making snowmen in the winter. We could be friends without things getting weird. But everything has a different meaning now that we're older. Now there are, like, *implications*.

3

It's so weird that school started two weeks ago. It feels more like two months ago.

It's also weird to think about how I used to be. Because I was nothing like I am now. Well. Maybe the core of me is the same. You know how there's always a part of you that stays the same, no matter how many other things change or how drastically you try to reinvent yourself? But I'm different now in one major way.

The thing about having an anxiety disorder is that you never quite fit in with everyone else. Not like that's a bad thing. But when all you want to do is function like a normal human being, not fitting in just makes your problems a million times bigger. Last year, I was antisocial and depressed and always thinking these negative things. Life kept moving all around me, but I wasn't really involved in any of it. I watched everyone else doing all of the things I thought I was supposed to be doing. Those things looked so easy for them, like joining clubs and doing the school play. But it always felt like such an act if I tried to fit in the way normal kids did.

"How's it going over there?" Dad says from his side of the table we're sanding. My dad makes furniture. Everything he makes is solid wood, which is expensive but lasts a lifetime. Several lifetimes, actually. He has studio space in town, but he also works at home. That's why there's this whole carpenter's setup in the garage. Sometimes I help him with things that won't ruin whatever piece he's working on, like sanding.

"Looking good," I report.

"Like I knew it would."

I love helping Dad. Whenever we're working on a piece of furniture, I just focus on what we're doing and my anxious thoughts calm down. It's part of my Cognitive Behavioral Therapy I learned from my psychologist last year. If I'm having anxious thoughts, I'm supposed to do something to redirect my energy until I relax.

We're using very fine sandpaper, and all you can hear is this soft *fffft-ffft* sound as we sand the table. Dad taught me how to use a very light touch and this special circular motion so the surface won't get sanded down unevenly.

"How's school going?" Dad asks.

"Good." *Fffft-ffft.* "We're already practicing for the winter concert in orchestra."

"Of which you'll be the star. You're concert mistress, right?"

"*Dad.*"

"What?"

"It takes years before that happens. Like maybe by the time I'm a senior I *might* get noticed."

"But you're so good already."

That's how my dad is. He's always super supportive. No matter how badly I screw up, he's always there to pick up the pieces of me. I think it hit him harder than my mom when they realized how messed up I was last year. I wasn't bipolar or insane or plotting to blow up the school or anything. I was just, like, *depressed*. A lot of people with anxiety get that way sometimes. For me, I think my obsessive negative thinking and worrying about things like stupid stuff I did or what people think of me just naturally made me depressed, as if my mind was breaking down from the stress of it all. Mom is always more comfortable talking to me when I'm feeling normal, but Dad reaches out no matter what. Let's just say Mom didn't talk to me much when I was at my worst.

But I'm better now. And I want everyone at school to know that I'm not a freak anymore. Except I'm finding out how hard it is to revise the previous version of myself. All of that energy Sterling and I had before school started with our improvement pact and reinventing ourselves has kind of worn off.

Dad hands me a new piece of sandpaper. "Anything else going on I should know about?"

"We're setting up an aquarium in chemistry."

"How is chemistry related to fish?"

"We haven't had that yet. I think it has something to do with pH."

"Ah. Sounds fun."

"I guess."

"You were working on your chem lab yesterday, right? Over at Nash's house?"

"Don't remind me."

"I thought you liked going over there."

"I do, but . . ." *Fffft-ffft.* "It's just, I'm totally lost in that class and Nash knows everything. His brain is like this industrial sponge that sucks everything in and keeps it trapped there forever. You can ask him anything and he'll totally know."

"Sounds like a smart guy."

"He's a freaking *genius.*"

Dad smirks at me in this way where he's thinking that I like Nash.

"I know what you're thinking," I say, "and it's not that."

"It's not?"

"No."

"Then what is it?"

"He's just . . . really interesting. Like . . . he collects bells? From all around the world?"

"Cool."

Mom opens the garage door. Dinner smells waft in. "Hey, you two. Time to eat."

"Be right there," Dad says.

"Now," Mom emphasizes.

"Gotcha."

Mom knows how lost in his work Dad can get. One time she told him to come in for dinner and he was still out here an hour later. He said it felt like only five minutes had passed.

Mom's job has always been being the mom, but over the summer she got a part-time job as a personal assistant. When I asked her what that was, she said some things about organizing travel itineraries and buying gifts, but I still don't completely get what she does. All I know is she's not around as much anymore and there are some nights when she has to work late. I'm already planning on going to Sterling's for dinner on those nights. Dad making my sister Sandra and me frozen waffles isn't the most appetizing.

Mom goes inside and I start cleaning up.

"Hey," Dad says. "I'm really proud of you."

"For what?"

"For this year. I know how hard it must have been to get better, and you did it."

"Thanks."

"You know I'm always here if you need anything, right?"

My throat feels really tight, so all I can do is nod.

4

"**D**on't even *think* about it," Nash warns me.

"Just a little?"

"No."

"Please?"

"That *no* part is nonnegotiable."

This is the third time I've been over at Nash's house. And it's the third time he won't let me open the window. He should know by now that I need air. But Nash has his room temperature perfectly regulated, and he hates when I threaten to mess it up.

"I'm just going to open it a crack," I promise. "You won't even notice."

"Then why open it?"

"No, I mean . . . *I'll* notice. But you won't."

"Are you implying that I don't notice stuff?"

We have this thing where he teases me and I pretend that I don't like to be teased.

"Why are you always trying to twist my words around?" I say.

"Why are you always trying to open the window when the air temperature is perfect in here?" he counters.

I give up. There's no way to win with this boy. Nash is smarter than me and I have no problem admitting it.

"Moving on," I announce. Then I notice that Nash has graph paper in all different colors. "Where'd you get that graph paper?"

"From the office."

"Which office?"

"The main office."

"The main office gives you graph paper?"

"No. I mean, yeah, but I do service credit there second period, so I get to take some."

"What do you do for service credit?"

"Just help out. You know. Like with the attendance sheets and stuff."

That's so weird. I never thought Nash would be the type of person to work in the office for credit. But of course it makes sense. We're only sophomores and he's already building his college applications.

"Where are we with the data?" Nash goes.

"Um . . . kind of lost?"

Nash glares at me over a stack of handouts. "I thought you finished the calculations yesterday."

"Yeah, see . . . the thing—I mean, that was the plan, to finish them. Yesterday. When I was making the data table. But . . . uh . . ."
How can I explain what an idiot I am? I'm not what you would call math-and-science smart. I'm good at things like creative writing

and art and music, and I like this psychology elective I'm taking, but math and science are just . . . not for me. No one told me there would be so much math in science. It's a total and complete letdown.

If I wasn't paired up with Nash for lab, I'd be toast. Right from the first lab report we did, he made it clear that everything had to be perfect or he wouldn't let us hand it in. So we've met twice already to do one stupid lab report that everyone else is probably waiting until the night before it's due to even start. Which is totally helping my chemistry grade, but that's not the only reason I like coming over to Nash's house. I admire how different and weird he is.

Nash harumphs. He flips through more handouts.

"I could try again tonight, but—"

"That's okay. Let's just get this over with." He gets up off the floor, where he was sitting across the coffee table from me, and goes over to his desk. Nash is the only person I know with a coffee table in his room.

He yanks a drawer open. A cowbell next to his computer tips over with a dull clank.

Nash has bells. A lot of bells. They're everywhere. Hanging from the ceiling and window frames, hanging on the walls, sitting on the bookshelves and desk, and jingling on a string tied to his dresser drawer handle. Nash collects bells from all over the world. He says he was inspired by his grandpa, who had a massive bell collection. Nash inherited his first bells from his grandpa after he died and he's been collecting them ever since. I guess it's a way for Nash to feel closer to him. He can pick up any bell and tell you exactly where it came from. And of course, there's a whole story that goes along with each bell.

He comes back with a calculator. "Okay, let's start with the first column. You have it?"

"Yeah." As I read out the data and Nash taps quickly on his calculator, I take peeks at his spider plant hanging in the window. It's a friendly plant.

One weird thing about me is that I feel affectionate toward some inanimate objects. Like, I love this special stripy pencil I have. Actually, it's not even that special. It came in a pack of five from Staples. It's just that I love the colors and widths of the stripes, the way the eraser rubs so smoothly, the rich quality of the graphite gliding across the page.

I'm convinced that I'm the only person who notices these things.

Or maybe I'm not. Maybe my future boyfriend is the same way. And maybe he's sitting in his room right now, wherever he is, wondering if he's the only one who notices these things. And I'm here. Just waiting for him to find me. Waiting for him to find out that I'm real.

5

We have a guest over for dinner. He's someone Mom knows from work. His name is Jack and his house is being painted, so I guess she felt bad for him and invited him over.

I bet Jack is wishing that someone had warned him about Sandra before he got here. He might have decided whiffing paint fumes in front of some lonely takeout was the better deal.

"But how can you say that?" Sandra asks Jack.

"That's not the way we speak to guests," Dad tells her.

Mom doesn't say anything. Lately at dinner, she's been getting into these zones where it seems like she's somewhere far away while we all sort of talk around her. But tonight she's agitated. She takes another bite of her salad. The iceberg lettuce crunches. If Sterling were here, she would be personally offended to be sitting at a table where the only lettuce in the salad is iceberg. Sterling is a fan of the tri-lettuce Parisian salad. But she never complains when she comes over to eat. She's compassionate like that.

Sandra tries again. "But . . . why do you think that?"

"There's no way this country's ever going to run on nuclear energy," Jack insists.

"Nuclear energy has the lowest impact on the environment—"

"But when nuclear waste disposal sites leak radioactive material, which they always do eventually, thousands of people can die."

"—of any energy source, it doesn't produce emissions that contribute to global warming—"

"Is reducing global warming more important than preventing people from getting cancer? Or making it easier for nuclear weapons to blow up the planet?"

"—and the water that nuclear plants use is never polluted, so—"

"It's not worth the risk."

"Be logical. How can you not agree with nuclear energy?"

There's no way you'd ever guess that Sandra is only in eighth grade. She acts, talks, and dresses older than me. And she's a lot more mentally stable. How fair is it that she got all the advanced genes?

The thing about Sandra is, she's the most confrontational person I know. She loves to debate. She's even in the pre-debate program. So by the time she hits ninth grade, she'll be like this crazy verbal attack monster unleashed. A monster with a really good vocabulary.

Sandra's been compiling evidence on alternative forms of energy because that's the topic the mini debaters are doing now. Which is how this fight with Jack got started.

Dad gives Sandra a warning look. Too bad he's not looking at Jack that way.

Jack's like, "So . . . your mom tells me that you're on the debate team?"

And Sandra goes, "Do you even know what uranium 238 *is*?"

Okay. Sandra just crossed the line. Having a "debate" with a dinner guest is one thing. Implying that the guest doesn't know what he's talking about is something else.

"Jack is our guest," Dad informs Sandra. "You're excused from dinner."

"But I—"

"*Now.*"

Sandra pushes back her chair so hard it almost falls over. "This," she huffs, "is *so* not fair."

I swear, she's such a drama queen.

Sandra stomps off to her room. Her door slams.

I glance over at Mom. She takes another bite of salad, looking at Dad.

He notices her looking. "What?" he says.

She just shakes her head. Then: "Can I offer you some more wine, Jack?"

"No, thanks. I'm good."

"I'd like some more wine," Dad says.

My parents hardly ever fight. They're always cracking jokes and laughing and holding hands like they don't realize how old they are. Except when they're not. Which is only in extreme situations. And even then, they make an effort to get along.

Mom has always kept more to herself. Like with those faraway looks she gets, or how sometimes she "needs a minute," which is code for going to her room and reading or watching TV alone.

Which ends up taking way more than a minute. I guess it's just a personality thing. She needs a lot of alone time, while Dad is the complete opposite. The more people around, the happier he is. You'd think that a marriage wouldn't work with two people being so different and all, but somehow it does. They just have this extrovert-introvert yin-yang thing going on.

Jack smiles at me. I don't smile back. There's something about him I'm not liking. What kind of person would argue with a thirteen-year-old girl about nuclear energy like that?

Jack goes, "I hear you're into photography."

"Yeah."

"You use a Nikon?"

I nod. "My dad gave me his old one."

Jack glances at Dad. "That's cool," he says.

Part of me wants to ask Jack why he was giving Sandra such a hard time. I mean, he's the adult. She's just a kid. But that's part of my anxiety problem. I keep all this bad stuff in and it makes everything worse. I just hate fighting. Sandra is crazy confrontational and it makes me want to avoid arguments whenever I can.

I'm expecting another lame question from this guy who obviously doesn't know how to interact with teens, but Jack just goes back to eating. We all do.

On the way to my room, I pass Sandra's door. Signs are plastered all over it, like READING MAKES YOUR BRAIN SMART and MAKE LOVE, NOT WAR and I ROCK AT PISSING YOU OFF. I think about knocking to see if she's okay, but I walk on by. We all need a minute sometimes.

6

Sterling and I do something together every Saturday night. It's our thing. It helps us feel slightly less pathetic that we don't have boyfriends. In our world, the ideal boyfriend would take us out every Saturday night. And the ultimate Saturday night date would be dinner and a movie. It's classic.

Don't get me wrong. It's not like we sit around complaining about not having boyfriends or anything. Getting boyfriends is part of our reinvention pact for this year and we're determined to finally make it happen. I feel like if I don't get kissed soon, I seriously might explode.

"Don't look," Sterling warns. She's blocking my view in case I refuse to follow directions.

"At what?"

"Tabitha is totally scamming on some random boy over there."

The Notch is the only good place to hang out when it's cold, so we usually come here a lot in the winter. But we haven't been here since June and I guess we missed it in some warped way, so we decided to make an appearance tonight. Until I went to camp this year, summers were all about lying on the beach (technically just this sandy area along the river) with Sterling. Which was probably really bad for us, even if we always used sunblock.

I love the beach. My dad and I go for beach walks and collect these polished stones that you can find if you look hard enough. I collect the white ones and he collects the black ones. On my windowsill, I have a glass bowl filled with all of my white stones. I also like to walk to the lighthouse and watch it in the twilight, glowing strong and bright. And a lot of people around here have boats or do windsurfing or waterskiing, so you can always get someone to take you out onto Long Island Sound.

The Notch has a big fountain in the middle of everything with four branches of shops sticking out from it. So the whole thing looks like a big X from overhead. There's a pizza place that plays movies on a big screen and has pool tables in the back. There's a gelato bar with a bocce-ball court. There's a movie theater with four screens. There's Cosmic Bowling and Happy Mart and Shake Shack, plus some chain stores.

A lot of kids from school are here tonight. Everyone likes to loiter near the fountain because you can scope out people walking by from all directions. We're sitting on the edge of the fountain and, from the way Sterling is blocking me, I guess Tabitha is probably sitting on the other side.

"She's not going to see me if I look," I tell Sterling.

"Just wait."

I open my bag from the music place. It has two CDs that I can't wait to play. The Mat Kearney one has at least one song from *Grey's Anatomy* on it. Scraping my fingernail along the edge where the industrial-strength packing tape is doesn't help it peel off. One time I was so impatient trying to pry a CD case open that it cracked. So I'm going for the calm approach this time.

"Okay," Sterling says. "Now."

First, I look the other way. I scan a group walking by, pretending to look for someone. Then I casually turn around, and there's Tabitha. Sitting on a cute boy's lap. Why does she always have to wear such tight shirts? But if you're pretty like Tabitha in a way where everyone agrees you're pretty, I guess you can get away with stuff like that.

"Who's she sitting on?" I ask.

"Maybe he's a junior?"

"Maybe he doesn't go to our school."

"How avant-garde."

The truth is, I'm jealous. Tabitha gets attention from boys all the time. It's like it's not even hard for her to talk to them. She just does it naturally. Where did she learn how? Or was she just born that way? If it's genetic, my DNA is definitely lacking that segment.

I want that. Not just to be popular with boys. I want a boy to love.

Julia and Evan come over and sit next to us. We're in the same group for global studies, so I say hey, but Sterling and I aren't really friends with them. I think Julia's mad at me. We kind of got in a fight the first week of school. It wasn't my fault. I was just shocked that Julia doesn't like to read.

When she told me that, I was like, "How can you not read?"

"It's boring," she went. "No offense."

"Have you read *Speak*? Or *Girl*?"

"No."

"So that's probably it, then. You're not reading good books."

"Like I said. They're boring."

"But good books aren't boring."

"To you, maybe. But not everyone has the same taste. There's other stuff to read besides books. Like magazines."

"That's not the same thing."

"Why not? It's still reading."

"Yeah, but books are . . ." How do you explain how books are nothing like magazines to someone who doesn't even read them? "Forget it." I had to give it a rest because she was obviously not interested in reading and that's just the way it was.

Julia's telling Evan about this webcast she heard last night.

"This guy comes on most nights at eleven. He's totally hard-core."

Evan's like, "Who is he?"

"He's anonymous. But he knows stuff about the school."

"Like what?"

"He totally shouted out this senior. She told everyone she had the flu, but she actually got a DUI."

"Maybe he just made it up."

"I don't think so. He *knows*." Then Julia tells him everything that was on the show last night. And how this guy's claims are legit and he has evidence and all. Apparently, he knows a lot about our school. "He obviously has, like, access to inside information."

"But how?"

"Maybe he hacked into e-mail?"

"You can't know all that personal stuff just from e-mail."

I'm getting bored with spying.

Then Sterling goes, "Hey, isn't that Derek?"

We both look at someone down by Shake Shack. He's far away, but I can still tell it's Derek. If I had a choice, I'd be sitting on his lap, just like Tabitha with her boy adventure.

But life's never easy when you need it to be.

Usually when we're here, Sterling makes me pick out a boy I think is cute. There's a decent selection of them because kids come over from other towns, since this is pretty much the only mall-type situation within a thirty-mile radius. Then she tries to get me to talk to some boy I don't even know. Sterling looks at it like this: If I want to make new friends and eventually have a boyfriend, I have to put myself out there the way she does. Not that being super friendly has helped her get a boyfriend. Sterling has as much experience with boys as I do. Which is approximately none.

Everything's easier for her, though. Sterling makes friends all the time. She does stuff outside of school, like cooking classes and yoga, so she's constantly meeting new people. She always has friends over. I try not to be jealous of her life, but it's hard. Sterling's all sophisticated with her social life beyond school, where there's freedom to be who you want. So she knows this whole group of people she actually wants to be friends with, instead of being restricted to the same wingnuts we're forced to live with year after year.

"Oooh, he's cute," Sterling says.

"I know."

"Not Derek. I mean, Derek's cute, but—" She points to another boy getting cookies at Mrs. Fields. "What about him?"

"That guy at Mrs. Fields?"

"Um-hm."

"He's like ten years older than us."

Sterling stares at him longingly. Then she's like, "Let's go try on jeans."

I groan. She's so tiny that trying on jeans is easy for her. For me, it's a whole different experience.

"You always think nothing fits you," Sterling goes, "but you're wrong."

"Which is why I only have three pairs of jeans?"

"You only have three pairs of jeans because you don't put enough time into building your wardrobe."

That's easy for her to say. If I were five two and skinny (but curvy at the same time), jeans would look as fabulous on me as they do on her. But I'm four inches taller and my hips do this weird puffing-out thing and my thighs are too fat and my butt just looks wrong. So finding jeans that actually fit me is a miracle.

I struggle to cram myself into the first pair of jeans I picked out. "Who designs this crap?" I complain. Sterling's in the next dressing room over.

"Yeah, really," she says. Just to be nice, I'm sure.

"Why does the waist always stick out so much in the back? Seriously. How hard is it to make jeans with a normal waist?"

"And why does my butt crack always have to be hanging out?"

"Maybe it's some obscure trend we didn't hear about."

"Uuuh! These jeans are corroded."

"They don't fit?"

"They're too tight."

"Maybe Tabitha would like them."

Sterling does her snorting laugh. When she laughs really hard, the snorting gets out of control.

I yank the jeans down over my hips and kick them to the floor. I'm not even bothering with the four other pairs. Nothing ever fits. There are some things I can't control and that's just the way it is.

7

Darius is a hard-core nerd.

You know the type. He's the kid who sits in the front of every class, raising his hand to answer every question. He wears glasses that are too big for his face. He has zero product in his hair. And don't get me started on what he's wearing. He's one of those overachievers who signed up for too many clubs during orientation week. If you say something wrong in class, he shouts out to correct you before the teacher can. He's the complete opposite of laid-back.

Darius is totally on the Harvard track and he's only fifteen.

I have mixed feelings about doing group work with him. It's good because he always takes over and does most of the work. But it sucks at the same time. Because, you know. He's Darius.

We've been working on this global activity for ten minutes. Everyone else is out of ideas. It's this project called Pay It Forward, where you have to think of how you can change the lives of three people you know. Then you have to write down your plan for how to help them. The idea is that they're not supposed to pay you back, they're supposed to pay it forward by changing the lives of three other people. If the chain works, it gets huge, and eventually thousands of people's lives could change. Ideally, the whole world would improve in major ways.

Of course, Darius is just getting started. So while he's writing down his ideas (and probably crossing out what the rest of us did), Julia starts talking about other stuff. She just had some bad highlights put in her hair. The highlights are so bad that I'm having a hard time focusing on what she's saying.

"Oh my god," she goes to me. "Did you hear it last night?"

"Hear what?"

Julia sighs all dramatically. "The *show*."

"No. I haven't heard it yet."

"Here." Julia writes something at the corner of her paper and rips it off. "This is his website. You *have* to start listening."

"Thanks." I take the scrap of paper. She's not the only one who's been talking about the show, so maybe I'll check it out.

Then Julia complains how she got no sleep last night. "My parents were fighting until at least three," she says. "They think if they go in their room and shut the door, it automatically sound-proofs whatever they do in there. Like, don't they know I can totally hear?"

"At least your parents still live in the same house," Evan says.

"That's nothing," Julia says. "Mine don't even talk to each other. The fight was an improvement."

"I'd rather have that than joint custody," Evan challenges. "Doing the room shuffle every weekend is so lame."

I stay quiet.

Everyone's looking at me expectantly. Except Darius, who's still frantically scribbling.

"That's harsh," I say to everyone in general.

Since it's glaringly obvious that my parents are normal, they dismiss me and go back to comparing whose parents are the worst.

I don't usually think about it, but when stuff like this happens I realize how lucky I am. My parents have a great relationship. They're my role models for what I want when I grow up. I don't know what I'd do without my dad. He's the one who always makes me feel better. He's the one who's there for me, no matter what.

My mom tries in her own way, but it's different. Like, she insists that we eat dinner together every night, which I know most families don't do. Apparently, I'm weird for having a normal family that does normal family things. But that's cool. I'd rather be weird and happy than normal and miserable.

On my way to psych, I see Derek with Sierra in the hall. My heart speeds up and I get all twitterpated, the same exact way I get every time I see him. It's especially severe when I run into him randomly like this, when I don't expect it. He's so cute. I spend a lot of time imagining what it would be like to be his girlfriend. But Sierra gets to be the lucky one.

Derek totally caught me staring at him in art the other day, which was potentially mortifying. Especially since he already caught me staring at him at Andrea's pier party. So now he probably thinks I'm a deranged stalker. But he was all sweet about it and just smiled at me.

That was a really good day.

Today, however, is majorly sucking. My homework took forever. It took me, like, three hours just to do the reading and questions for English. My brain is totally fried. I need to unwind or I'll have noisy brain all night. So at three minutes to eleven, I decide to hear what everyone's been talking about.

I get out the scrap of paper where Julia wrote the webcast guy's site. The site doesn't give any clues about who he is, though. It just says that he's called Dirty Dirk and it gives the link to his show. There's a backlog of listings starting in August. It's kind of amazing that kids were already talking about this guy when school started.

I click the link and there's a countdown to eleven o'clock. When the show comes on, it's obvious that he's using some voice enhancer thing so no one can tell who he is.

"Welcome to another night of All Talk, No Action. I'm your host, Dirty Dirk. I'm dark, I'm dangerous, and I'm downright dirty, so be warned that there's parental advisory stickers slapped all over this." Some vaguely familiar heavy metal blasts from the speakers.

Then Dirk's back on. "You all have issues you want to share with the world, so let's get to it. For our new listeners out there, you can shoot your questions, comments, and concerns to me whenev. Contact info's on my website. For those of you who've been with me from the start, thanks for hanging in. Hope I'm not boring you too much."

If he only knew. Does he have any idea how many people talk about his show every day? I even saw one kid passing around his iPod with the shows downloaded in case anyone missed the night before. Apparently, that was the night Dirk harshed something severe on how detention is unconstitutional.

"Here's one from Hopeless in Hicksville. 'Dirk, you gotta help me out, bro. I'm going crazy in this Podunk town. What do you suggest before I die of boredom?' Yeah, that's tough. We all feel you, dude. How many times can a person hang at the Notch and have it still be fun, right? Wait, don't answer that."

I like this Dirk guy. He's real. And from the other e-mails and IMs he reads, it's obvious that all of the kids writing in go to our school or at least live around here.

"Look, man," Dirk goes. "We're all sinking in the same boat here. We're all bored and desperate and waiting for something to happen. Waiting for life to get better. Waiting for things to change. Waiting for that one person to finally notice us. We're all waiting.

"But we also need to realize that we all have the power to make those changes for ourselves. Yeah, I'm the last one who should advertise about taking control of your life. I talk big and act like a dork most of the time. But it doesn't stop me from hoping I can be different. We all can change the way things are. Maybe not as much as we want to, but we can at least make things better."

I swear, it's like he's talking directly to me. How does he know what I've been dealing with? He makes it sound like I'm not the only one who feels so lost. And I already know I'll be listening to him every night.

8

Sometimes when I feel anxious, I can focus on things like developing my photos or practicing violin or writing on my wall, and I have the power to calm myself down.

But not always.

Like today. It's just one thing after another. So far I've had to endure (not necessarily in chronological order) the following atrocities:

1. My alarm didn't go off. Something happened to it in the middle of the night. So this morning I had to rush through my shower, which meant that I couldn't shave my armpits. That annoyed me more than it should have.

2. I left my English report at home. This would be the report that's worth, like, half our grade for the mark-

ing period. Could it happen with some sketchy global homework? No. Of course not. It has to happen with a life-or-death major English report.

3. The most embarrassing thing happened in geometry. I thought I knew the answer to this superhard question and Mr. Wilson was saying how if someone answers it correctly they'll get extra credit. But no one was raising their hand because it was too hard. So I raised my hand and I answered the question wrong. But that wasn't the embarrassing part. The embarrassing part was when I got inspired with this false sense of confidence from being the only one who tried to answer the superhard question and then I totally spaced on the easiest question in the world after. Not only did I get it wrong, but my answer was so far out there that someone laughed at me.

4. At lunch, I sat on a piece of ham.

5. My pen ran out during the chem quiz and I didn't have an extra one in my bag. I didn't want to ask Nash for a pen because I'd have to turn around and it would totally look like I was cheating. So I tried to motion to the girl next to me if she had another pen I could borrow. But then Mrs. Hunter saw and she thought I was cheating. So she came over to my desk and I tried to tell her that I was just asking to borrow a pen but she wasn't listening. She was all, "We

can talk about this after class," and she took my quiz away.

And, really, all I had to do was go up to Mrs. Hunter after and tell her what happened. But when the bell rang, all I wanted to do was leave. I didn't even look at her as I walked right out the door. Which, of course, was stupid, since now she probably thinks that I really *was* cheating and that's why I left so quickly.

But whatev.

At least I survived and I'm over at Nash's house now. I'm liking it here more and more. I feel really comfortable, almost like it's an extension of my house or something. So we have this routine now where I come over to his house every week to do our lab reports. But today, even this is less than perfect. Because it's too stuffy in here.

"Can I open the window just the tiniest bit?" I go.

"Okay," Nash says.

"Okay?"

"Yeah."

Dang. He must really feel bad for me. I told him all about my horrific day. It's so easy to talk to him. Sometimes it's even easier to talk to Nash than Sterling. I mean, of course I can tell Sterling anything, but she's usually preoccupied or doing five other things while I'm talking to her. With Nash, I can tell he's really listening.

Nash goes over and opens the window. His room feels a lot better with fresh air in it. I wonder why he doesn't know that.

I also wonder why there's always socks on his floor. I'm like,

"What is it with boys and socks?"

"You mean with leaving them around?"

"Yeah. What's up with that?"

"I don't know." Nash glances around at his floor, where I've already noticed two stray socks. That don't even match. "I never really thought about it."

"But your hamper is right over there," I inform him, gesturing toward the closet in case he doesn't know.

"Um-hm. The floor is closer."

"Wow."

"We're like a completely different species, right?"

"I never knew how serious it was."

"Oh," Nash says, "it's serious."

I suddenly get this glimpse of how Nash would be if he'd quit schlepping it all the time and got some style. And if he changed his attitude. He should really just relax and be more friendly. I mean, he's nice to me and he always helps me in lab, but I've seen him interact with other people and he could definitely use some social tips.

There's all these random computer parts and wires and mechanical-looking pieces of things stacked in one area of the floor. "What's all that?" I ask.

"It's for Dorkbot."

"Did you just make that up?"

"No! It's a robotics group."

"Seriously?"

"Yeah. We do strange things with electricity. And there's a competition every year where all the best projects are presented. Last year this guy invented a way to play music like a video game."

"How?"

"You had to see it. He had these bubbles filled with music and . . . it's hard to explain. It was wild."

"It sounds cool."

"It was. Hey, if I make it to the finals this spring, you can come with me."

"Dorktastic!"

"But you're not allowed to say that."

"Deal. So what's your project?"

"Oh, it's way too early to know. There are several different ways I can go with it."

"I can't wait to see what you do."

"Yeah?"

"Of course!"

We do our lab report for a while, listening to Arcade Fire and eating Twizzlers. Nash goes, "Can I ask you something?"

"What?" Did he read my mind before about being in desperate need of a fashion overhaul?

"Actually, it's more like . . . I need your advice. About something."

"Okay." Yes, you do need a whole new haircut and, yes, I can tell you exactly how it should look.

"It's about . . ." Nash jiggles his leg up and down. I can't believe he's nervous about this. I mean, it's no big deal. "There's someone I might . . . like."

"Oh." That's the last thing I ever thought he'd tell me.

"So . . . yeah. But I'm not exactly the most outgoing guy."

That's the understatement of the century. I've seen Nash talk to one girl at school besides me when it wasn't for class-related reasons. And that was only because her chair leg was on his backpack strap. He's always so shy, unless he's helping someone. That's why I still can't figure out how he got the guts to ask me over for lab reports. I guess if it even remotely has to do with school, Nash isn't nervous.

"You could say that," I admit.

He nods.

"So you want me to . . . tell you what to do?"

"Ah . . . I'm just not sure what to do about it."

"Does she know you like her?"

"No."

"How do you know? Maybe she's already picked up on your vibe."

"I don't think so."

"Who is it?"

"I can't tell you."

"Why not?"

"I just can't."

"So I know her."

"No comment."

And that's when it hits me. Is this Nash's way of telling me he likes me? But he's too shy to tell me directly so he's hoping I'll see through this thinly disguised attempt?

I go, "So . . . you're too shy to tell her to her face, right?"

"You could say that."

"Well, there are other ways to tell her without saying it."

"You mean like . . . write her a letter?"

"Exactly."

"Doesn't that reek of seventh grade?"

"That's why it works. It's cute in a retro way. She'll love it."

"Really?"

"Definitely. I mean . . . depending on what you write."

"What do you suggest?"

There's no way I'm helping him write a love letter to me. How weird would that be? "Um . . . just, you know, be honest about how you feel. Tell her why you like her and stuff."

"Hmm." Nash thinks this over. "I guess you don't want to help me write it or anything."

"I think this is one of those things you just have to do on your own."

Nash nods, still thinking. "Yeah. I guess you're right."

We go back to doing our homework, but now I can't concentrate. What if he likes me? What am I going to do? There's no way I could like him back. He's *so* not my type. I have no idea whose type he even is. But I know for sure he's not mine.

9

My aunt Katie is the coolest person I know. Even though she's my mom's sister, you would never know they're related. While Mom is all quiet and contemplative, Aunt Katie is the complete opposite. She's totally fun and spontaneous. She'll be sitting at home watching a movie and the next thing you know she's driving to New York because she has to see this trellis in Central Park that some characters were walking under, *right that second.*

Aunt Katie is a topiary designer. Which basically means that she gets paid serious money to cut people's bushes into animal shapes. Plus, she owns her own company for topiary design and landscaping, so people actually work for her. Not that this makes it any easier to believe that she's thirty-two, because she acts like she's sixteen. But in a good way. She shops in the juniors section and even borrows my clothes sometimes.

"Okay," Aunt Katie says. "What do you think of this one?"

I examine my laptop screen. "Hmm."

"Be honest."

"He's cute, but . . ."

"But what?"

"It's just . . . what's that on his arm?"

Aunt Katie leans in closer to the screen. "Where?"

"Right there." I point to this thing over his wrist that looks like a tattoo.

"Whoa." She squints. "It looks like a damaged cartoon character, right?"

"Is that a Muppet Baby?"

"Um . . . yeah. Next!"

Aunt Katie joined eHarmony a few weeks ago. She's sick of going out with guys who don't want a serious relationship. They act all interested at first, but then they eventually tell her they don't want to get serious. Which is ridiculous because Aunt Katie is a hottie. Plus, she's totally sweet and interesting and smart and funny. I don't get why guys don't want to be with her. It has to be a problem they all have in common.

My parents met at jury duty. According to Dad, it was love at first sight. Mom took a little longer to realize this. They hit it off the first day they met, sitting in a room the whole time and talking because they never got selected to serve on the jury. So they never had to think about things like online dating. Not that it was even possible back in the day.

Aunt Katie clicks on the name OCTAVIO.

"Cool name," I say sarcastically.

"Be nice."

When Octavio's picture comes up, I see a big problem right away.

"So?" she asks.

"I don't think so."

"What? Why not? I think he's cute. And he's a dentist."

"That's half the problem already. Dentists are sadists."

"No, it means he has an actual career instead of living at home playing video games every night in the same room he grew up in."

"He has no lips."

"You're talking crazy talk."

"I'm serious! Look!"

Aunt Katie leans in again. "I see definite lippage."

"Where?"

"Uh, where his mouth is?"

"Yeah, if you like fish mouth."

"Fish mouth? What the heck is fish mouth?"

"What Octavio has."

"No way."

"How does he kiss with no lips? Like . . . what, he just presses up against the girl's mouth and hopes for a suction effect?"

Aunt Katie clicks to close his picture. "Has anyone ever told you that you're too picky?"

"Oh! So *that's* why I've never had a boyfriend. Thanks, I get it now."

She laughs. "Yeah, like you should have so many ex-boyfriends by the time you're fifteen."

I glance out my window at the river, which looks totally bored. It's all flat and gray.

"I only need one of these guys to be the one," Aunt Katie says, scrolling down her list.

"How many of them have you met?"

"Just three. But I have a good feeling about one of them. . . ." She clicks on the name BILL. When his picture comes up, I understand where the good feeling comes from.

I go, "He's freaking gorgeous."

"He looks even better in person."

"Shut *up*."

"Seriously."

"How many dates have you guys had?"

"Two. But we're going out again this weekend."

"How tall is he?"

"Umm . . ." Aunt Katie scrolls back up to his stats. "Six one. And he actually is. Not like some of these other guys who say they're six-whatever and then you meet them and they come up to your chin."

"Go Bill."

"Yeah. Well. We'll see."

"I thought you liked him."

"I do. But I still have to go out with other guys."

"Why?"

"I have to make sure he's the right person for me. I have to see who else is out there, you know? And he's probably seeing other people, too."

"Isn't that weird?"

"In a normal world, yeah. But with this online dating stuff . . . it's typical."

"Weird."

"It takes time to be sure of someone. And to be sure of yourself when you're with them."

"What do you mean?"

"If I'm with the wrong guy? I don't feel like myself. I make irrational decisions."

"Irrational decisions like . . . making a judgment about someone based on their appearance?"

"Yeah. Wait, no. Sometimes you can do that and it's not irrational."

"Like if someone has a serious case of fish mouth?"

"You know, there *are* other things to consider. Like personality? And how a guy treats you?"

"Okay, but what's the point of all that if you're not even attracted to him?"

"I hear you, but . . ." Aunt Katie scrolls down. "Sometimes attraction grows. Remember Campbell?"

How could I forget Campbell? The night Aunt Katie showed up with him for dinner I was like, *This is a joke, right?* Because Campbell was so not her type. He just wasn't what you would call attractive. He was more like remotely passable. But Aunt Katie loved him. So my initial opinion of him gradually changed and I ended up thinking they were perfect for each other. They were together for a long time, almost two years.

The thing was, I liked Campbell. He was really funny. He'd make me laugh so hard that my stomach was killing me and my face hurt. And he'd always bring over a gift for me, like a Beanie Baby or a Slinky or one of those big lollipops with rainbow colors all swirled together. I'm still not sure why they broke up. Maybe Aunt Katie decided that she liked him more as a friend.

"But you guys broke up," I say.

"I know. But it was still the best relationship I've ever had."

"Really?"

"Absolutely. And at first I wasn't even attracted to him. But after a while, I thought he was so cute."

I try to understand what she means. It's a stretch. "So you're saying that someone can become cuter over time?"

"Um-hm. But it's not that they change. It's that *you* change."

Aunt Katie shows me some more profiles. She wants to get married so badly. I can definitely relate. We're both waiting for that one person who will make our waiting end.

When I think about how different my life will be when the waiting is over, it's scary and exciting in that new-experience kind of way. Where you've never been there before, but you know you're in the right place. Because your real life, after all this time, is finally starting.

10

There's this rivalry between the orchestra and band geeks. Everyone in band thinks they're just as talented as us. But actually? It's way harder to play a string instrument. That's because if you don't put your fingers in the exact right places, whatever you're playing will sound heinous. It's nothing like being in band and playing a wind instrument, where all you have to do is press some buttons or slide some lever around, so the notes are never off-key. How simple is that? But the band geeks still think they rock hard.

Ignorance is a problem in this school.

I share a music stand with Andrea. Last year I was second violin, sixth chair, and now I'm second violin, third chair. My goal is to be concert mistress by senior year. That would be so sweet, with the entire orchestra following my cues. I have a lot of work to do if I'm ever going to get there, though.

We're playing this impossible piece with thirty-second notes and all these random rests. So it's not the best day to be cracking up. Like the way I've been doing for the past five minutes.

Once a week we have full orchestra. That's when the band comes over to our room from their room and we all play a few pieces that we've been working on together. I like it better when it's just orchestra. The intimate chamber music is calming. But with the band geeks all invading our territory, it's a riot of loud toots and squeaks.

The trumpet solo blasts out this rude honking noise. I try to stop laughing. But the honking noise makes it even funnier.

Andrea whispers, "What's so funny?"

There's no way I can tell her and not get caught, so I whisper back, "Tell you later."

Mr. Silverstein has radar for these types of things. Anyone who's even remotely not paying attention usually ends up having to play the next ten measures alone. Which is like the most horrendous form of torture ever. We're all scared of him. So when Mr. Silverstein focuses his laser-sharp stare on me, I freeze up. He doesn't say anything.

We start playing again. The thing I've been laughing at is still funny and I can't get it out of my head.

It happened last period in chem when we were learning about pressure on gases. There was this diagram of a flask and some other stuff on the board. Mrs. Hunter was doing a practice problem. She labeled parts of the diagram and we were copying it down. Because, you know. We're going to use this information later in life. So Mrs. Hunter was standing in front of the diagram and lecturing and I looked up at her and she was standing right on the other side of this arrow that was labeled GAS EMISSION. And the arrow was pointing right at her butt. It was the funniest thing I'd ever seen in class.

I'd like to be able to look back on that class and say, "Yeah, I was mature about it. I was just like, whatev, and kept on copying the diagram."

But that's not how it was.

I laughed so loudly that someone walking by in the hall actually looked in to see what was going on. Every single person in the room turned to stare at me. Mrs. Hunter stopped lecturing and stared at me. Behind me, Nash coughed.

No one else was laughing.

How could they not think this was funny? Could they not see? But then I figured out that I was the only one who could see exactly where the arrow was pointing from the angle where I was sitting. And that's why I was making an ass of myself, bordering on the edge of hysteria.

Everyone kept staring at me.

And then Mrs. Hunter gave me a crushed look like she expected more from me. She started lecturing again.

I could feel the sharp point of a folded note Nash was pressing against my back, but I didn't turn around. I've never been in heavy trouble and I didn't want to start then over something so stupid.

So when the image of the gas emission arrow pops into my head again, I laugh. The shaky motion yanks my bow across the

E string. There's this loud squeak when we're supposed to be playing a quiet part.

Mr. Silverstein motions for everyone to stop playing. And there's that laser-sharp stare again. Directed right at me.

My face burns.

Mr. Silverstein goes, "Marisa. Would you care to let us in on the joke?"

I shake my head. My face burns hotter.

"No?"

I shake my head again.

"That's a shame. I could really use a good laugh today."

I look at my sheet music.

"In fact," he says, "I insist you tell us."

I glance up at him to check if he's serious.

He's serious.

There's no way I can tell him. It's too stupid and embarrassing. And if Mrs. Hunter finds out what I was really laughing at, because of course Mr. Silverstein would tell her, I'll be toast.

"It's nothing," I tell him.

"Really? Nothing?"

Please don't make me play ten measures by myself.

"Well then," he says. "I guess you can contemplate the hilarious nature of nothingness tomorrow in detention."

So unfair. There's no way I can get detention over this. I'm not the kind of girl who gets detention. I'm not one of those burnouts who's disruptive and a loser and everyone treats her like a reject. Teachers think those kids are the biggest waste of time.

See, right now? I'm supposed to be using my relaxation techniques to remain calm. If I let this get to me, I could turn into an emotional wreck, reliving this scene over and over until I'm convinced that no one will ever accept me as a functional human being. That's why I'm supposed to control any crazy thoughts by reminding myself that they're unrealistic. And I'm supposed to do it right when they happen, or else the thoughts expand until they're too huge for me to tame them.

Except it's not really working. I'm convinced that everyone thinks I'm deranged. It's like whenever I hear someone laughing, even if they're all the way on the other side of the room, I'm convinced that they're laughing at me. It's one of my irrational assumptions that come with having an anxiety disorder. And sometimes I feel like nothing will ever make them go away.

Andrea gives me a sympathetic look. I know she feels bad for me. But everyone else is looking at me the same way I'd be looking at anyone who did what I did. Like that person is a total freak.

11

No matter how outrageously wrong life gets, I can always count on Sterling to make me feel better. She's my rock. And in a different way from my dad, since I'd be mortified to admit things like this to him. I don't want him to think I'm an idiot. So after school, I go over to Sterling's and try to recover from the humiliation of orchestra.

"At least you didn't have to play ten measures by yourself," Sterling says. "How embarrassing would that have been?"

"I know. But detention? Me?"

"I guess you really have changed."

"Oh, yeah, into a total loser who gets detention for laughing. I can't believe this is my life."

"Here. Try this." Sterling takes a tiny piece of something off a tray filled with other tiny pieces of something. They look like mini versions of the finger food that was at this wedding I went to, except these are more colorful and complex. She puts the strangest one on a napkin and slides it across the counter to me. "You'll feel better."

"What is it?" I ask, secretly horrified. I'm suspicious of tiny food. And it has a little green sprig sticking out.

"*Amuse-bouche.*"

"A what now?"

"It's French. It means 'mouth amuser.'"

"You made these?"

"Of course. There are four different kinds—want another one?"

I watch the *amuse-bouche* on the napkin in front of me.

"What's wrong?" Sterling says.

"Isn't it . . . sort of . . . small?"

Sterling laughs. "That's the point. It's a pre-appetizer. You're supposed to eat it before the hors d'oeuvres."

"Oh. It's cute."

The green sprig dares me to eat it.

Over at the stove, Sterling suddenly gasps.

I go, "What's wrong? Did you burn yourself?"

"I just remembered! Guess what I have for later."

"I don't know."

"Guess."

"I really have no idea."

"Guess anyway."

Sometimes Sterling can be so annoying. But she can also be a lifesaver, so I let her get away with it. She was my lifeline last year. She was always there for me when I needed her, even when it was really late and she had to get up for school the next morning but I didn't because I was too messed up to go.

I'm waiting for a good guess to arrive at my brain. "Um . . ."

"The box set of *My So-Called Life*!"

"Get out!"

"I know!"

My So-Called Life is this show that was on in the mid-'90s. It was only on for one season, but it's supposed to be genius. I read about it on a blog and we've been hunting it down ever since. It was one of those random DVD releases where you could only find it on eBay for, like, five hundred dollars.

I'm like, "Where did you find it?"

"It just came out again."

"Sweet!"

Sterling holds up a small pan and goes, "Like my new sauté pan?"

"Totally. Is that the Calphalon one?"

"Of course. What kind of ramshackle operation do you think I'm running over here?"

She really is the one who runs things. Sterling's mom works for the United Nations, so she's constantly traveling. Sterling's alone a lot of the time. Her grandma lives down the street, so nights when Sterling's mom is gone her grandma sleeps over. I'm usually not here when she comes over, but we've played cards a few times. She's really nice.

"Aren't you so excited about the DVDs?" Sterling shouts.

"Absolutely."

"I heard Jared Leto is so smoking hot in this you can't even look at him without your eyes burning off."

"Okay, but um . . . we should only watch one disc."

"Why?"

I have this thing where I can't wait to see what happens next, but I can't watch all the episodes right away. Because once you watch them, they're, like, *gone*. Forever. It will never be new again and that first time can only happen once and you will never again have that feeling of excitement at seeing fresh eps. And that's a sad and lonely feeling.

I'm all about the anticipation. Sterling knows this.

"Oh, no," she complains. "This isn't your weird obsession about saving some to watch later, is it?"

"Maybe."

I'm expecting Sterling to try and convince me that we need to watch the whole season tonight. But she's just like, "You're so weird."

I glance at the *amuse-bouche*. The green sprig quivers.

"Are you ever going to eat that?" Sterling says.

I decide not to let my irrational fear of tiny food prevent me from tasting something fabulous. So I try it. And it's delicious. And then we get psyched for the year again and creating the lives we want and I feel all the excitement that's been missing since the day I got back from camp when we made our reinvention pact.

The excitement is still there when I wake up the next day. I had a tingly dream where I was with my future boyfriend. It was the best feeling ever. I didn't even know you could feel that intense in a dream and still remember it when you woke up.

So I'm having a really good day. Right up until I see Jordan coming down the hall.

This is it. This is when I'll know for sure.

Nash took my advice about writing a letter to the girl he likes. We had this discussion about how there's no way he can give it to her in person. He'd be way too nervous and then he'd get embarrassed because she'd see. But if he had a friend give her the letter instead, then he could watch from down the hall or something and not have to be directly involved. That way, if she doesn't like him he wouldn't have to stand there and find out the hard way, right in front of her, while her eyes tell him everything he never wanted to know.

So Nash decided that his friend Jordan would give her the letter. And that it would be today, in the hall, at her locker, before lunch. Which is now.

I see Jordan walking down the hall, which is always easy to do since he's the tallest sophomore. He has this slow, loping walk. I'm glued to the floor, pressed back against my locker, watching him. I just know he's coming over to bring me the letter. Because I'm obviously the girl Nash likes.

My insides tremble with nervous excitement. Jordan gets closer.

And then he stops across the hall about ten lockers away from mine. And he gives a letter to Birgitte. Birgitte, as in Tabitha's equally skanky best friend.

The trembly nervous thing inside of me turns into nausea.

I know I shouldn't keep watching this. I know I should just turn away, get my lunch money and my notebook for my next class out, and go to lunch. But I can't. I can't stop watching them.

Birgitte rips open the envelope and takes out a folded piece of loose-leaf. She stands there reading it while Jordan waits, glancing down the hall. I follow his glance. I can barely see to the end of the hall, but I know Nash is there. Waiting to see if he should be happy or suicidal.

While Birgitte reads, Jordan fidgets. He takes his keys out of his pocket and jiggles them around. And then this really messed-up thing happens.

Birgitte starts laughing. Right in his face. And she doesn't stop.

Jordan drops his keys. I look down the hall to see if Nash is watching, but he's too far away to tell. I'm sure he can hear her laughing, though. If there's someone in Australia who can't hear, I'd be shocked.

This is all my fault. I'm the one who gave Nash the advice to do this, and now look. But I thought we were talking about me the whole time, so maybe it doesn't count. What's he doing liking Birgitte? Doesn't he know how lacking she is?

Birgitte says something to Jordan. He looks too shocked to say anything back. Then she shuts her locker. She shoves the letter in her bag and walks away.

Jordan sees me watching him. I pretend I'm looking for someone else across the hall. Of course no one's there.

And that's when I realize why I was sort of hoping the letter was for me, even though I don't like Nash that way. After my waiting for someone to like me for so long, this was the first time that a boy might have actually liked me for real. Instead of it always being a fantasy.

12

If Derek weren't going out with Sierra, I'd think he was flirting with me.

We've only been in art for five minutes and he's already come over here twice. One of those times was to borrow my pastels, when he totally knows there are loads more boxes stacked up on the supply table. Plus, he was all smiling and extra polite about it. Which is not exactly how I would describe the way he interacts with me under normal circumstances.

Derek comes back over with the pastel box. He holds it out to me and goes, "Thanks, Marisa."

"Sure." I take the box from him. I'm doing a sunset scene. Someplace warm and tropical where you don't have to rush through life because time doesn't matter so much.

I blend some blue and pink pastel streaks together with my thumb. Derek watches. When I look up, he goes, "I like what you did with that."

He likes what I did with what? The whole scene? The colors? The blending? I have no idea what this boy is talking about or why he's even talking to me, so I just go, "Thanks," and keep working.

"Where did you learn to blend like that?"

Um, is he serious? Because I can't tell. I mean, he *looks* serious, but he could just be setting me up for some kind of twisted humiliation. He caught me staring at him those times, so he probably knows I like him.

"It's a natural talent," I say.

"Is that Fiji?"

"What?"

"Your scene." Derek points to my paper. "It looks like someplace tropical."

Wow. He really does get what I'm doing. It's not like I've drawn any palm trees yet, so how would he know unless he actually does?

"Yeah," I go. "It is. Someplace tropical, I mean. Not necessarily Fiji."

"I'm definitely getting Fiji." Derek inspects my paper. "*So* Fiji."

I smile. I can't help it. No one's ever gotten anything about my drawings.

He smiles back.

And he still has a girlfriend.

I stop smiling and take out another pastel.

"See ya later," Derek says, all smiling again. It would appear that he's definitely flirting with me.

But why? He's never talked to me before. So why now? He must be attracted to my new magnetism. When Sterling gives me tips for making new friends, she always says that people pick up on your energy and respond to you in subconscious ways. So if you exude positive energy, people will be nicer and they'll want to be around you more. Maybe Derek's picking up on my energy.

And that's exactly what I want. For certain people to be on my wavelength. Because those are the people I want to be friends with. Or more than friends with.

Except I don't want to be more than friends with boys who already have girlfriends. That's just tacky. And boys who scam on some other girl when they already have a girlfriend? What does that say about them? But the thing is, it's Derek. I don't even remember the whole first week of art because I was staring at him so hard my concentration blocked out everything else.

I can't get him out of my mind. So after dinner, I lock myself in the bathroom that I share with Sandra. I always practice violin in here. The acoustics rock. Something about how the sound waves bounce off the tile.

I've only been practicing for a minute when Sandra pounds on the door.

"Can you *not*?" she yells. "I'm trying to read!"

"So read downstairs," I yell back.

"No! I want to read in here!"

"Well, I'm sorry. I can't help you."

"Quit playing!"

"I can't! I have to practice!"

"*Mom!*" Sandra screeches. I hear her door fling open. Then she pounds down the stairs, thumping like an elephant. She always walks like that. It drives me crazy.

This piece I'm practicing feels really delicate. Like how a kiss would sound. Not that I'd know about kissing. I went to one dance in seventh grade and kissed one boy for one second. That's it. And even when I was in the middle of kissing him, I wasn't counting it as my first real kiss. It was more like a practice kiss. And the fact that I knew it was a practice kiss while we were kissing basically means that I shouldn't have been kissing him.

I focus on the music. I have laser-sharp focus.

Bang bang bang!

"Get *out*!" Sandra yells.

"No!"

"I can't hear myself think!"

I unlock the door and whip it open. "Both of us have to live here, you know," I inform Sandra.

"It's been the joy of my life."

"So you'd better get used to it. I'll never be first violin if I don't practice."

"Fine, but why do you have to practice in here?"

"It sounds better."

"That's such a lame reason!"

"It's still my reason!"

"This sucks!" Sandra flings herself across her bed. "I have to read!"

"What's going on in here?" Dad says. He's standing in Sandra's doorway, doing the Dad Grimace he always gets when we fight.

We both start yelling at the same time. I'm like, "I have to practice and this is the only good place—" and Sandra's like, "She won't let me read!" and Dad's like, "Hold on! One at a time. Marisa."

"You always take her side!" Sandra wails.

"I'm not taking sides," Dad clarifies. "I asked her to explain first. Then you can go. See how that works?"

Sandra scowls.

"Like I was saying," I go, "I have to practice and it sounds better in the bathroom."

"There's a reading quiz tomorrow!" Sandra yells.

"Okay," Dad says. "Is this the only place you can read?"

"Unbelievable! Why don't you ask *her* to move?"

"Marisa." Dad turns toward me. "Is this the only place you can practice?"

"No, but it's the best place."

"And this is the best place for me to read," Sandra interjects.

"It seems we have a conflict here," Dad concludes. "How do you girls think we should resolve it?"

He does this sometimes. Instead of being Harsh Dad, he likes to be Friendly Dad. Which is cool when you know you're wrong, because then he takes it easy on you and you don't really get in trouble. But this time I know I'm right. I just want him to tell Sandra to shut up and stop being such a baby about everything.

Sandra and I glare at each other.

"Tell you what," Dad says. "Why don't we compromise?"

I groan. The translation of *compromise* is *no one gets what they want*. It's all about trying to make someone else happy instead of yourself. But they're not happy either because it's a compromise instead of what they really want.

"Marisa, you can practice for half an hour here, but then you have to move downstairs. Is that fair?"

No. "Yeah."

"And Sandra, why don't you either read downstairs for now or do something else?"

"Fine," she huffs. "But it's your fault if I fail my quiz."

"No one's telling you you can't read," Dad tries to reason with her. "I'm just saying—"

"Yeah, Dad," she interrupts. "I get what you're saying."

Sandra always thinks Dad takes my side. She's convinced that he loves me more and always has. Which is ridiculous. But when Sandra has an opinion, that's it. It's carved in stone. You can't convince her anything else is the truth, even if it obviously is.

13

Nash and Jordan organized our school's First Annual Wii Championship. Sterling and I decided to go watch. So far, all that's happened is a lot of hyper boys are swinging themselves around and looking like fools.

It's in the gym. Everyone's sitting on the bleachers. Some kids from student council are setting up another big projector screen next to the one already there. Apparently, playing on one screen isn't exciting enough.

Derek's here. He's sitting in the next section, one row down. The corner of my eye is like glued to his face, waiting for him to look at me. It tingles with anticipation.

I saw him right when we came in. That's why we're sitting where we are. We came in and there he was and I was like, "I *so* know where we're sitting." But I didn't go right up to his section or anything. That would have been too obvious. Over here is much more subtle.

Suddenly, Derek turns to look in my direction. I do that thing where the boy you like is watching from over there so you pretend to have a riveting conversation with your friend, all exaggerated hand motions and animated expressions.

"What's wrong with you?" Sterling says.

"Did you see that?"

"See what?"

"He looked over!"

"Who? Derek?"

"Of course Derek!"

"Oh. I didn't really notice."

"How could you not have noticed?"

"Maybe because I'm not obsessed with him like some people?"

"I'm not obsessed."

"Really? How many times have you told me about him flirting with you in art?"

"Well excuse me for noticing." I don't know why she's acting like it's such a crime to be excited that a boy might like me. I mean, *really*.

"You *do* know he's going out with Sierra, right?" Sterling goes.

"Of course I know that. Everyone knows that."

"So then why are you so interested?"

"I'm not that interested."

Sterling looks at me.

"I'm not!"

"Okay," she says. "Whatever."

Nash gets up to play. He's playing against Julia. She's the first girl who's gone up.

The gym door bangs open and a group of four girls comes in, squealing all loud. Most of the people watching the tournament don't even notice, they're so glued to the screens. But I notice. Because Sierra is in that group of girls.

I was so relieved when I saw Derek here without her. I was hoping that his flirting with me plus being here without her would equal him liking me. And maybe not liking her so much anymore. But Sierra runs across the floor and clatters onto the bleachers right over to Derek.

She kisses him. I look away.

"Do you feel like getting out of here?" Sterling says. "It's kind of lame."

"Yeah." I can't be here another second.

Sterling leads me out to the vending machine area and buys a pack of Chuckles. We sit on the floor. Sterling takes out a yellow Chuckle and chews it.

My brain won't shut up. It's doing that noisy brain thing where the horrific scene with Derek kissing Sierra is playing over and over, making it impossible for me to focus on anything else.

Focus on something else. Do not let obsessive thoughts take over your life.

"Why don't boys like me?" I go.

"Boys like you."

"Not the ones I like."

Sterling eats a red Chuckle.

"Look," she says. "You'll find who you're supposed to be with. Just because all the boys here are buttwipes doesn't mean your boyfriend doesn't exist. He's probably just somewhere else, is all. He'll find you."

"But *when*?" I can't take it anymore. The waiting. The wanting.

Something inside me snaps. I hate myself. I hate that I have to deal with this. I hate my life. And I hate how I can't count on anyone to be completely there when I need them, exactly the way I need them to be.

I feel horrible in my room all night until Dirk's show comes on.

"Did anyone else watch *America's Slackers* tonight?" Dirk goes. "What's up with these inane reality shows taking over the airwaves? And now we're celebrating stupid people who sit around all day doing nothing? While awesome shows like *Freaks and Geeks* get canceled? What's wrong with this picture?"

Dirk rules. I've been wondering the same exact thing. Especially ever since Sterling and I watched *My So-Called Life*. It just doesn't make sense that so many quality shows get taken off to make room for more of the same crap.

"It's like that old *Sesame Street* segment. What was it? 'Which of These Things Does Not Belong?'" He tries to sing the song that goes with it, but he can't remember the words. "Nice—just got an e-mail that's saying the song is called 'One of These Things Is Not Like the Others.' Oooh . . . and a link to Cookie Monster singing it! Sweet! Let's have a listen, shall we?"

Then Dirk plays the song. You'd think it would be dorky with Dirk playing some old *Sesame Street* song and all of us in our rooms, listening. But it's not. Sometimes when I feel stressed, I revert back to my old Judy Blume books from middle school or reruns of shows I used to watch in fifth grade. These things are comforting. They remind me of who I was before life got so complicated. And they give me hope that maybe one day I can get back to that peaceful place again.

14

"Do you think it matters whether you drink warm water or cold water?" Nash wants to know.

I'm used to his non sequiturs by now. It's amazing how we've become such good friends since school started, after years of hardly talking. Things like this make me think that anything can happen.

I say, "Yeah, it matters. Who wants to drink warm water?"

"No, I meant room temperature. Like if you leave a bottle of water out instead of putting it in the refrigerator."

"Oh. Is that what room temperature means? Thanks for clearing that up, Dr. Obvious." Nash feels the need to explain the most obvious concepts to you. Sometimes in great detail. Which is *so* annoying.

He was the same way in chem today.

We were doing this lab and the partners at the next table didn't get how to do part of the procedure. So they asked Nash for help and he explained some stuff. But then later, for this really simple question about ratios, Nash started telling them all this super basic stuff that even a fifth grader knows.

The girl was like, "Yeah. We know."

"Just trying to help," Nash said.

"Do you think we're stupid or something?" she shot back.

"No, I was—"

"Then why are you talking to us like that?" her partner accused.

I know Nash didn't mean anything by it. But if you didn't know him, I could see how it would be easy to take him the wrong way.

"Well?" Nash is asking me.

"What?"

"Do you think it matters to your body?"

"Why would your body care what temperature water you drink?"

"Here's what we know: Your body's standard temperature is ninety-eight point six degrees. So, if you drink some really cold water that's like fifty degrees below your normal body temperature, wouldn't that be a huge shock to your system?"

I flip a few pages ahead in the project we're working on. "What page is that on?"

"It's not part of the project. I'm just wondering."

That's another thing about Nash. He wonders about the most random things.

"I don't know," I say. "I've never thought about it before."

"Let me know if you come up with a theory."

"Oh, don't worry. You'll definitely be the first."

Three hours and two breaks later, the project is done. The middle of October is stressful enough with the first marking period ending and report cards coming out, without having this huge chem project on top of everything. At least things are sort of getting better. I actually feel like I can contribute when we work together now. When we first started doing lab reports, Nash was so smart and I didn't know anything. I felt like such an idiot.

I hate it when other people feel like they have to do all the work or answer questions for me because they know I'll never get it. That happened a lot back in my dark days. When I got really depressed, I'd tune out in school. Or sometimes not even go. And my mom would let me stay home because she didn't know what else to do. Dad would come home early and play Uno with me and try to get me to talk about what was wrong, but I usually didn't feel like talking much. Mainly because I didn't know how to explain it. So I was absent a lot and I'd miss what was going on in class. Whenever I had to do group work, everyone would be looking at me like, *You're supposed to know this. Why are you being so dense?* It was really embarrassing.

But now I feel like I'm actually getting some of this stuff. And I think we did a really good job on the project. I smile at Nash, all proud of us.

"What?" he says.

"Nothing."

"No, what?"

"Nothing. It's just . . . I think we're a good team."

Nash stops stapling pages together. "I do, too."

I smile some more. Nash looks terrified.

"Are you okay?" I ask him.

"Um . . . yeah . . ." He gets up from the coffee table where we were working. "I got some new bells."

"Oh, cool. Let's see." He shows me a string of tiny bells hanging from the window frame. I shake them. They sound light and tinkly. "They're cute."

Then Nash launches into this long, complicated description of where they're from and how he found them and why they're significant to a certain culture halfway around the world and—

"Hey, Nash?"

"Yeah?"

"They're cute."

"Thanks."

And then we're just standing there, with no one saying or doing anything. He's just looking at me.

It's weird. For the first time with Nash, I feel like I need something to say. I'm all, "So . . . whatever happened with . . . the letter?" I was going to say, *Whatever happened with Birgitte?* But Nash never told me it was for her and I don't want him to know that I saw her laughing at Jordan.

"What letter?"

"You know . . . the one you wrote for . . . um . . ."

"Oh! That. Nothing. She didn't feel the same way."

"That sucks."

"Not really. It's actually a good thing. I was more interested in someone else anyway, so . . . "

"Who?"

"Just someone."

"So why didn't you give it to her?"

"Practice," Nash says. "You think I'm going to bust out my best material in the preliminary round?"

I'm not buying this whole thing where Nash is trying to blow it off like it's no big deal. Liking someone and having them reject you is a *major* deal. I'm learning how to read Nash and he's not very convincing. But this is what he wants me to believe and the truth is humiliating, so I let it go.

"So, um . . . I guess we're done," I say.

"Done?"

I point to the coffee table. "With the project."

"Oh. Right. Yeah, we're done."

"I think it's really good."

Nash says, "Marisa . . ." And then he moves closer to me. As if he's going to kiss me or something.

Oh my god.

Nash is going to kiss me.

I *knew* he liked me!

I turn away from him.

"What's wrong?" he says.

"I'm not . . . I don't . . . Were you trying to kiss me?"

"That depends."

"On what?"

"On why you didn't let me."

This is really hard. How do you tell someone who likes you that you don't feel the same way about them? No one wants to hear that. It's devastating.

But I have to tell him.

"Nash, I don't . . . you know . . . like you that way."

"You don't?"

"No. Did you think I did?"

"I don't know. It just seemed like you did."

"Well, I don't."

"Yeah, I'm picking up on that."

"Sorry."

Nash skulks to the other side of the room.

I have to know exactly why he thought I liked him. It's so strange because I totally don't. "Did I . . . do something? To make you think I liked you?"

"You could say there were some clues."

"Like what?"

"You always like to come over, for one."

"To get our work done. And because we're friends."

Nash picks up the big cowbell from his desk. He clanks it a few times.

"So that's it?" I say. "I like coming over, so you thought I liked you?"

"No, there's more than that. You just seem . . . forget it."

I still have no idea what he's talking about. But he already feels bad enough, so I decide to let it go.

Nash is like, "I can't believe this is happening again."

"What?"

"*This.* Rejection."

"I'm sorry. But I didn't—"

"Yeah. You can't force yourself to feel something you don't, right?"

"That's not what I was going to say."

"If it's worse than that, I really don't want to hear it."

"I was going to say that I didn't mean to hurt you. You just . . . surprised me, is all."

"You surprised me more."

We both stand there, looking anywhere but at each other.

"Okay," he says, "this is awkward."

"It doesn't have to be. I still want to be friends."

Nash snorts.

"Don't you?" I ask.

"Do you really think that's possible?"

"Why not? I mean, it'll probably be weird for a while, but—"

"It would be more than weird for me. I'm the one who likes you."

"So . . . what are you saying?"

Nash shakes his head. He still won't look at me. "I don't know yet."

This is so unfair. Why did he have to go and ruin everything? How could he think that I liked him? Did I give him any indication that I did? No, I couldn't have. Because I don't like him. I still want to be friends with him, though. We have to still be friends.

Only . . . what if we can't?

November-January

15

Here's the bad news: It's been two weeks since the non-kiss incident and Nash and I haven't seen each other outside of school at all. He said it would be better if I didn't go over to his house the way I usually did for our lab reports. So now we're doing the parts of our lab reports separately and putting them together to hand them in, the way everyone else does.

Here's the good news: Dad almost finished building my dark-room. He converted a closet that we never use in the basement, and now it's all mine. I'm totally psyched to start using it, but the sink needs a new part or something. So I have to wait a few more days.

Unlike Mom, I'm not into the empty house thing. If I want to get away from everyone, I just go to my room and sequester myself in the fortress. But when no one else is home, it just feels lonely. Like now. It's like the lack of people in other parts of the house makes my own space feel empty. And I can't concentrate on homework because my brain keeps insisting on being noisy.

I go downstairs, trying to decide what to do. I don't feel like reading or going online or watching anything.

We have thick photo albums on the living room bookshelf. When Sandra and I were little, my mom was obsessive about taking pictures of us. But she doesn't really do that anymore. I'm not sure why. So when you look at the albums, there's tons of pictures of us until we're about twelve and ten, and then only a few after that.

I pull out one of the middle albums from when I was about seven. We had a dog named Buttons. I loved him so much. When he died, I cried for weeks. I thought I'd never feel better again. My dad kept saying things like "time heals all wounds," but I didn't believe him.

Flipping through the pages, I remember that my mom has this whole box of old pictures she never put into albums. The albums are supposed to be for the best pictures, but she has a lot more pictures she thought weren't good enough for other people to see. Those are the ones I always thought were way more interesting. I think that box is in her closet.

My parents' room always feels so decadent. Of course it's the biggest bedroom in our house, since they were here first and all. They have this awesome walk-in closet. I go in and search the shelves for the box, but I can't find it anywhere. I check my dad's side. I know my mom stores random stuff there because she has way more clothes and there's no room on her side. I still can't find it.

Something feels strange about Dad's side of the closet. It's just . . . off. Emptier, somehow. Every two years, my mom makes everyone clean out their closet and put things in piles to donate. Maybe she just cleaned out Dad's stuff. But her side of the closet looks the same. Plus, she would have told me to do mine because she always donates everyone's things at the same time.

I check again. Something just feels wrong.

And, suddenly, I remember something Sandra told me a few weeks ago. Supposedly, she saw Dad leaving with a box of stuff when he thought no one was home. I told her it was probably just some work stuff he was taking to the studio, but Sandra didn't think so. Maybe Dad did his own cleaning this time.

I eventually find the box of photos on Mom's side of the closet. I lift it off the shelf and sit down with it on the floor. Sifting through photos of family picnics and trips to Vermont and all of us hiking and my parents looking like kids swimming in the river, all of these memories come rushing back at me in one big wave. This intense emotion washes over me, but I don't know what it's called.

I'm not sure how much time passes. Minutes or hours, it's all a blur. I just know that by the time I'm finished looking through all of the photos in the box, I can't believe how lucky I am. I have parents who love each other and love me. I have a nice house and enough money for things I want. I have everything I need.

So I don't get why I was all depressed before. My psychologist said how my body can't help feeling bad because of genetics and environmental factors, but I disagree. I think you can decide how to feel and then make yourself feel that way, if you're determined enough. I probably just didn't try hard enough to be happy. But it doesn't mean that I can't try harder now.

16

All I can think about is Derek.

I can't sleep. I think about him for hours, lying in bed at night.

I can't eat. Even eating two crackers is an accomplishment.

The ability to pay attention in school is a distant memory. I take notes, but I don't know what I'm writing. Teachers talk, but I don't hear them.

My noisy brain has mushed into Jell-O brain.

It's always like this when I'm crushing on a boy. I can't even read before I go to sleep anymore, which has always been my thing. I open my book, I read one or two sentences, and then it's like . . . my mind just wanders off and I think about Derek and I can't stop. And if I'm trying to read at school, all I can do is stare at the page because I can't concentrate enough to read the words. No matter how hard I try.

I'm falling in love with a boy who already has a girlfriend.

It's not entirely my fault. Derek is making it impossible not to notice him. He always sits with me in art now. Before Halloween he just started sitting at my table, right across from me. So now that we've been talking every day and he's right in front of me every day, he's all I can think about.

Since I have art first period, I can't eat breakfast anymore. My stomach is tied up in knots, knowing that not only am I going to see him really soon but he's actually going to sit with me. And talk to me. Like he actually likes me.

When Derek comes into art in his puffy North Face coat, I pretend I'm busy getting paint. I sneak looks at him. I spill paint on my sleeve.

I'm even more nervous when we start working.

"Where do you see yourself in ten years?" Derek asks me. We're doing watercolors for the next two weeks. He's painting a landscape and I'm working on a sheet music design for my binder.

"Random," I say.

"Thank you."

"Um . . ." No one's ever asked me that before. I don't really know what to say. I might want to be a professional photographer, but I'm not sure. And I don't know if I want to live in the country or the city. Growing up in a town like this is so boring it makes you want to leave, so I definitely want to move away. It's weird because when people come back to visit from college they always say how nice it is here. I guess it's a better place to visit than it is to live in. At least, if you're a teenager. "I'm not really sure yet. Not here, though."

"I feel you." Derek mixes different colors together to get another kind of green. "This place blows."

"So where do you see yourself?"

"Away from here, like you. Running my own landscaping business."

"Get out!"

"I know it's dorky, but I don't care."

"No, my aunt has her own landscaping business!"

"Dude."

"She's a topiary designer, and her employees do the landscaping part."

"Okay, now *that* is random."

"I know!" This is a total sign. How random is it that he likes landscaping, which I've never heard any other kid say they like as a career choice?

We talk nonstop for the rest of the class. I tell him all about how cool Aunt Katie is.

Derek says, "Sounds like it would be awesome to work for her."

"You should!"

"I'm not sticking around after graduation—"

"I meant next summer. She sometimes has interns. It's unpaid, but at least you'd learn a lot."

"That would rock! Can you ask for me?"

"I can ask if she's taking interns, but if she is you'll probably have to apply like everyone else."

"No special treatment for friends, huh?"

So we're friends now? I wasn't sure what Derek was thinking about us, sitting together like this. If he thought of me as more than an acquaintance.

And could he ever think of me as more than a friend?

"Well," I say, "I can make a recommendation."

"Sweet."

Then Derek tells me all about landscaping and the things he loves best about it. The different types of stone used for walkways and walls. Drawing plans and deciding exactly where a pool should go. How to create rock gardens or elaborate fountains. His passion is contagious. Not like I want to bust out and design a labyrinth, but his excitement excites me. It's awesome to connect with someone who feels passionate about things the way I do. So many kids I know are so blah about everything.

Blah sums up chemistry these days. It's just not the same anymore. Nash used to pass me notes and whisper stuff and sometimes, when Mrs. Hunter was taking attendance, I'd turn around and draw on his notebook. Now we're pretending that we were never friends or something. I'm lucky if he says more than two words to me the whole class. And when we have to work together for lab, all Nash wants to talk about is what we're supposed to be doing. I tried to bring up the non-kiss incident a few days ago, but he wasn't trying to hear it.

"I just want everything to be the way it was before," I said.

"We all want things," Nash went.

"But why can't we go back to how we were?"

"You can't go someplace that doesn't exist anymore."

I know he's right. Things have changed. There are implications. But I want Nash to know that just because he likes me, it doesn't mean we can't be friends anymore.

Whatev. Now that Derek's talking to me, maybe I don't have to miss Nash so much.

17

Every fall, our town has this Harvest Festival where booths are set up with things that people make—stuff to wear or eat or add to a knickknack collection. There are also some booths with games, like the ones we have on the boardwalk, but dinkier. And there are contests, like a pie-eating one (which is gross and therefore I never watch it) and knitting and Sudoku. The festival is always on the river, which I don't get because it's the first week of November and getting cold, and some years it's totally freezing. But it's traditional to have it there, and there's not much you can do about tradition.

I told Sterling I'd help set up her booth. She has her famous heart cookies, plus some cakes, pies, and brownies that she's been baking with her grandma all week. Every year, people tell her that she could run a catering business, her desserts are so tasty.

It's a sunny day and not too cold. Everyone's out in their new sweaters. The air smells like red leaves.

All of Sterling's cookies are individually wrapped in opalescent cellophane, tied with different colored ribbons. Her booth has skinny tree branches crisscrossing over the table, which we're hanging the cookies on.

Sterling drops a cookie. It cracks into pieces on the table. She kicks the table.

"Damn! That's like the fourth one."

"It's okay," I go. "You made tons."

"It's not okay."

"I'll buy that one. I don't care if it's broken. It still tastes the same."

Sterling's all tense.

"Don't worry," I say.

"I'm so stressed-out. My back is killing me."

"What about yoga?" I ask. "Can't you use some of your relaxation techniques?"

"Yeah, right, like I'm still doing yoga."

"You're not?"

"Can you really see me sitting still long enough to concentrate? You're supposed to empty your head to increase consciousness. So I'd be in this triangle warrior pose or whatever and all these thoughts about stuff I had to do kept interrupting. It's like the more I tried not to think about them, the more they would keep bothering me."

I'm not exactly surprised. "Okay," I go, "but what's wrong?"

Sterling points in the direction of the ring toss booth. Ricky's over there, cheering on a player.

I'm like, "Oh."

"Since when is the ring toss booth set up across from mine?" Sterling has been baking for the Harvest Festival for a few years, and before that her grandma ran the booth. It's an understood rule that everyone's booths are always set up in the same places.

"I can cover here if you need a break."

"That's okay."

Ricky is this boy Sterling went out with a few times over the summer. She went on and on for pages about him in the letters she wrote to me at camp. She really liked him, but it didn't go anywhere. He just stopped calling her. And it's not like she can confront him at school, because he's in college. She never knew why he stopped calling her. She tried to find out, but he never responded to her e-mails or messages. I have a theory, but I would never say it to her face.

Here's another example of how John Mayer explains the answers to all of life's problems in his songs. Sterling's life can be explained by "Daughters." We totally just did this in psychology elective. See, Sterling's dad is completely out of the picture, so she has no example of what a healthy relationship looks like. We learned how if you have abandonment issues, you can get clingy. And boys don't like clingy.

This wasn't really an issue last year, since not that many girls had boyfriends. But now things are changing. You can see it. It's like the force of boys and girls hooking up is a visible entity.

"When are you going home?" Sandra demands. She totally came out of nowhere. I hate when she sneaks up in my face like that.

"Later," I go. "Why?"

"Mom wants to talk to you."

"About what?"

"She didn't say."

"Well, she has to wait. She knows I'm helping Sterling all day." Sandra eyes the heart cookies.

"Want a cookie?" Sterling asks her.

"No, thank you. I'm off processed foods."

"Oh," Sterling goes. "Why?"

"If you knew what free sugars did to your system, you wouldn't be asking me that."

Sterling gives me an amused look. Sandra's been on this deranged health kick since school started. I seriously doubt it'll last much longer. I mean, no cookies? How ridiculous is that?

"Just tell Mom I'll be home later," I say.

"If I see her," Sandra goes. "You're not the only one who's out." She huffs off toward the farmers' market stand.

"What's with the attitude?" Sterling says.

"Puberty."

"Oh, right. I remember that."

At this game a few booths down from Sterling's, we watch a little girl trying to climb across a twisty rope ladder without falling onto the bubble mat. They have these huge Hello Kitty prizes, so there's a line.

I look around some more.

"Who are you looking for?" Sterling goes.

"No one."

"Oh, so you're not looking for Derek?"

Actually, I was looking for Nash. I was hoping that if I saw him today, things could get back to the way they were between us. If I only see him at school, things will definitely stay weird.

"Yeah," I say, "because I'm so interested in watching him and Sierra together. It's the highlight of my life."

"You might not have to for much longer." Sterling turns back to watch the girl, who falls off the ladder and bounces onto the bubble mat.

"What do you mean?"

"Nothing. Just that I heard something. But it's unconfirmed, so . . ."

"What?"

Sterling smirks in her I've-got-gossip-and-it's-extra-juicy way. "Someone in French Club, who shall remain nameless, told someone else that she heard they might break up."

"Who?"

"Hello! Derek and Sierra!"

"Why?"

"I don't know. That's just what I heard."

What if . . . Are they breaking up because of me? There's no way. Derek just realized I exist like three seconds ago. I'm sure he only likes me as a friend. Anyway, it's probably just a rumor.

When I'm walking home later, I see Nash out on the dock. Maybe we can finally talk.

I go out to him. There's a cold breeze coming from the river, blowing and then fading away. The water is all ripply.

"Hey," I go. I pull the sleeves of my sweater down over my hands. "Why weren't you at the Harvest?"

"I have too much work," Nash says.

"You're supposed to do something fun on weekends. Like relax a little? Hang out with friends?"

"Yeah, well, I have all this Mathlete prep. Our next competition is in four days."

I sit down next to Nash. Our feet dangle over the water.

"How's your Dorkbot project going?" I ask.

"Coming along. Sort of." Nash goes back to flipping through pages of a massive math textbook.

I get the feeling that he doesn't want to talk to me. Or see me. But I don't care. I just care about getting our friendship back. So I sit with him on the dock with the sun getting lower in the sky, just so he knows I'm still here.

18

So the rumors were true. Derek and Sierra broke up.

No one knows exactly how it happened. There are like twenty different versions of the story going around. Who broke up with whom and where they did it and why. But none of that matters now. The only thing that matters is that I finally have a real chance to be with Derek.

Maybe he'll ask me out in art. He has to assume that I know they broke up, because everyone's talking about it. Only, I've been waiting for him to say something all week and he hasn't.

After another grueling art class in which Derek doesn't ask me out, I'm ready to give up. I'm so stupid to think he would like me. It's not like I haven't seen Sierra. It's not like I can compete with her.

I walk out with him anyway.

Derek goes, "See ya."

I go, "Okay."

And that's it.

"He likes you," Andrea says in orchestra. She saw him walking out with me after art. "I can totally tell."

"Really?"

"Definitely."

"Because I thought so, but—"

"Do you like him?"

"I guess." I can admit this to Andrea because she's my friend. And we've been getting closer this year, dealing with the stress of the looming winter concert and the relentless scrutiny of Mr. Silverstein.

"Are you gonna tell him?" Andrea says.

"I don't think so."

"Why not?"

"Well . . . didn't they just break up like a week ago?"

"Something like that."

"So isn't it too soon?"

"Not from what I've heard." And then Andrea tells me all this stuff about how Derek and Sierra were always fighting and how it was obvious that they were way wrong for each other. "They were so incompatible."

"Then why were they going out?"

"Have you seen her at the beach?"

"Yeah."

"There's your reason."

Would I really want to be with someone who goes out with girls just because of how they look? Or was there more to their relationship than Andrea knows? Probably. Or else why would he be interested in me? I'm not as pretty as Sierra. I don't think I'm that pretty in general. I mean, some people say I am, but I don't really believe them.

Eileen is this girl in our violin section who sometimes acts strange. Andrea and I have to concentrate really hard not to let Eileen distract us. Whenever we're playing an intense part of a piece, Eileen gets this majorly focused look and sways back and forth with the music. I admire her soul, but it's a bit much. And she's always so serious. I don't think I've ever seen her smile. She keeps her eyes glued to either her sheet music or Mr. Silverstein the whole time. Nothing can distract this person. She's a laser.

It's a full orchestra day and I'm already getting a headache. I peek at the girl who plays the triangle. It's so weird that you can actually *play* the triangle. Like, other than just dinging it now and then. But she's actually pretty good.

There's a piccolo solo for a bunch of measures in this piece we're practicing today. During the solo, this superhigh note comes out like a scream. Eileen jumps a mile off her chair. She knocks the rosin off her music stand and it shatters on the floor.

I sneak a look at Andrea. She's cracking up. It always makes us laugh when Eileen gets so jumpy over nothing.

We're still laughing in the hall after orchestra. Sterling comes over to us.

She's like, "Hey."

We calm down enough to say hey back. But then we look at each other and crack up all over again.

"What's so funny?" Sterling says.

"Nothing," Andrea says.

"No, what?" Sterling presses.

"It's just something that happened in orchestra," I explain. "You had to be there."

"Yeah," Andrea adds. "You had to be there."

Sterling looks annoyed. I'm not trying to make her feel left out, but I know it's coming off that way. I try again.

"Something happened with Eileen, is all," I say. "It was funny."

"So why can't you tell me?"

Andrea and I glance at each other. How does Eileen jumping out of her chair because a piccolo squeaked equal funny if you weren't there to see the nuances of it all?

"Whatever," Sterling goes. "Laters." All we can do is watch her leave.

"What's her problem?" Andrea goes.

I don't know what her problem is. She's acting like a totally different person.

Thought: Maybe she hates Andrea? Did Andrea do something to her that I don't know about? Sterling definitely holds grudges.

So that night, I IM Sterling.

f-stop: why did you walk away like that?
frappegrl: i didn't walk away.
f-stop: yes, you did.

frappegrl: no . . . that was called i had to go.

f-stop: why were you acting all weird?

frappegrl: why were you laughing at me?

f-stop: what? when?

frappegrl: uh, today? in the hall? with andrea?

f-stop: i told you. we were laughing at this stupid thing. it was
    nothing.

frappegrl: yeah, yeah, from orchestra, i know.

f-stop: it's true!

frappegrl: then why wouldn't you tell me what happened?

f-stop: it was one of those you-had-to-be-there things. you know
    how those are.

frappegrl: yeah, i do. i also know you can totally tell someone
    about them. the other person might not laugh as hard as
    you, but they can still get it.

f-stop: i'm sorry we didn't tell you. it was stupid.

f-stop: you still there?

frappegrl: ☹

f-stop: now what's wrong?

frappegrl: since when are you & andrea so tight?

f-stop: since last year. you know we have orchestra together.

frappegrl: just because you have a class with someone doesn't
    mean you have to be best friends with them.

f-stop: we're not best friends. you're my best friend. do you not
    like andrea anymore or something?

frappegrl: i just felt left out.

f-stop: okay . . .

This is so lame. Sterling's in a tizzy and I didn't even do any-thing. So what if Andrea and I are getting to be better friends this year? Sterling has tons of other friends. Why should she care who I'm friends with? I mean, she's always needed a lot of attention from me, but she's always there when I need her so it's a two-way street with us. Except today it feels more like a dead end.

19

I always thought my sweet sixteen party would be a rager.

    I used to have all these fantasies about what my life would be like when I was in high school. Sterling and I liked to imagine how our junior prom would be, exactly how our dresses would look and everything. I thought I'd be doing all the fun stuff I've always heard I should be doing by now, like having a boyfriend and going to lots of parties. But now that I'm here, I have to say that I'm less than thrilled with reality.

I told my parents that I don't want a party this year. It just seems so elementary school. Not that it stopped them from doing a family thing. Because when I come down for dinner, the dining room is all decorated with crooked streamers and balloons. The table is set with paper birthday plates and cups and napkins. There are party hats on the plates.

"Happy birthday!" everyone yells together. Aunt Katie is here and even Sandra looks tame.

"Hey," I go. "You guys didn't have to do this."

"We wanted to," Dad says. He comes over and hugs me. "You only turn sixteen once, kid."

I sit down. The grown-ups beam at me. I put my party hat on. I am too old for this.

I'm also bummed, because it's obvious that Derek doesn't like me and he's never going to ask me out. It's been two whole weeks since the breakup and still nothing's happening. And then there's how weird everything is with Nash. And Sterling spazzing out over nothing. Let's just say life has been better.

Now that I'm sixteen, I have to get my working papers. Sandra and I get an allowance, but Mom and Dad insisted that we have to work part-time to save for college. As thrilling as the prospect of dishing fro yo is, I am *so* not looking forward to working.

Everyone knows that the most important part of a birthday is the cake. So when Mom brings out a carrot cake, I'm crushed. People are waiting for me to blow out the sixteen candles, but I just look at their glowing, wavering tips like I'm unfamiliar with this ritual.

"What's wrong?" Aunt Katie says.

"Is this carrot cake?" I go.

"I thought you liked carrot cake," Mom says.

"No," I say. "I hate carrot cake."

"I love carrot cake!" Sandra yells. Then, all quiet: "Not like I'm having any."

How could Mom mix up our favorite cakes? Mine is chocolate with vanilla icing. Mom knows that. Or at least she used to.

Mom goes, "I'm sorry, sweetie. I don't know where my mind is these days."

"Whatev," I say. "It's no big deal." I know I'm being a brat. I know it shouldn't matter. But one little thing can set me off like that.

Dad tells one of his rambling jokes that takes like twenty minutes to get to the punch line, and usually by then you forget why it's supposed to be funny. I get that he's trying to make it all better, the way he always does. He's like the only person I can count on these days.

No one lets me help clean up, which is fine by me. I collapse on the couch and click through some channels. Nothing's ever on. I'm half watching TV and half watching Mom give Dad a bag of garbage to take out. He takes the bag and then reaches for her hand, but she pulls away from him. It's the first time I've ever seen anything like that happen. I was so preoccupied with feeling sorry for myself all through dinner that it didn't register how they weren't touching then, either. That never happens.

Dad leaves to take out the garbage. Aunt Katie goes outside after him. How many people does it take to put a bag of garbage in the garbage can? And what the hell is going on around here?

As if all that's not weird enough, the next day in global is just as strange. I'm expecting Darius to do all of our group work, as usual. If I were him, I'd be mad that I did everything and everyone else got credit for it. But Darius doesn't think like that. He thinks like this: If I want the work done right, I have to do it myself. It's better than having everyone do some of the work and getting a lower grade. So usually we're all set.

Except we're not. Because Darius isn't even pretending to do the work, like some other groups are. He's staring off into space.

I look at him while he's still staring. He's completely changed. He's wearing those dangerously low-riding baggy jeans that all the hard-core slackers wear. He has earbuds hanging around his neck, which you're not supposed to have out in class. His eyes are all glazed over, like he doesn't even care.

My life is so *Twilight Zone*. When did all of this happen?

20

I got this job at Claire's about two weeks ago right after Thanksgiving, which was so lame. I mean Thanksgiving was lame, not the job. Actually, my job is lame, too. But Thanksgiving was tense. There's definitely something going on with my parents. They hardly even looked at each other all night. And Sandra refusing to eat half of what Mom cooked didn't help.

Claire's is at the Notch, so I can walk here from school. I work two days a week after school, plus weekends. I get a discount on everything, which is sweet because I love their rings and glitter eyeshadow.

Today's one of those days when I don't feel like talking to anyone, but I have to because it's part of my job. When you're in retail, you don't exactly have a choice about social interaction. And I've always told myself that I would never turn into one of those snarly cashiers who bites your head off for breathing. People at least deserve to buy their ultra-trendy jewelry that will go out of style next month in peace.

I'm not even paying attention when the next customer comes up to the counter. "Did you find everything okay today?" I ask without looking up. It's an automatic reply to someone coming up to the counter. We're required to say that, just like we're required to say, "Hi! Welcome to Claire's!" when someone walks in.

This time, the customer doesn't say anything back. So I look up from the book I'm reading (which we're totally not supposed to do, but it's slow) and there's Nash.

"Not yet," he says.

"Hey! I didn't see you come in."

"Reading under the counter again?"

It's this thing I do when no one else is around. There's a guy up front watching the door and someone else is stocking the racks with new bracelets. But there are no customers. I always sneak a book and read when it's quiet. If I sat here and did nothing, I'd fall asleep.

I'm psyched that Nash came to visit me. He came in one other time. It was my second day here and Nash was passing by with Jordan, on their way to Shake Shack.

"Of course," I admit. "Do you want me to die of boredom?"

"Not especially."

And then we're just kind of looking at each other with nothing to say. I'm beginning to think that this weird vibe will always be there between us, no matter how hard I try to make it go away.

"Um . . . I can't stay long," Nash goes.

"Okay . . ."

"I just came by to pick something up for someone."

"Oh. This *someone* person wouldn't happen to be a girl, would she?"

"How'd you guess?" He smiles a little.

"I'm skilled like that. If you could be more specific about the *something* part, I might be able to suggest something the someone might like."

"Well, I was thinking earrings."

"Not a necklace? Because there's this really nice one I can show you. That, you know. This *someone* might like." I do a big-eyes thing like, *Hmmm! Who can this someone be?*

Nash says, "It's for Rachel."

Which wipes the smile right off my face. "Oh." I see Rachel every day at school. We're in the same geometry class. I had no idea Nash liked her.

"You know we're going out, right?"

"Um . . . no. I didn't know that."

"Yeah, well . . . she wears a lot of earrings, so I just thought . . ."

"No, yeah, earrings sound like a better idea."

"Do you like the earrings here?"

"They're okay."

"Which ones are your favorite?"

"Um . . ." I move out from behind the counter and go over to the earring displays. "I like these." I hold up a pair of silver swirly ones. "But I guess it more depends on what she likes."

"Yeah . . . I really don't know."

"Doesn't she wear a lot of big earrings? Like these." I pick a pair of big gold hoops off the wall. "They make a certain statement."

"Like?"

"Like I'm a loud extrovert who wants everyone in the room to notice me." I can't believe I just said that. I sound like a total bitch. And for some reason, I'm having a problem with saying the name *Rachel*. Why can't I just be happy for my friend? Why do I have to be such a freak about everything?

"Rachel isn't exactly like that," Nash says.

He's right. Which is the suckiest part of this whole thing. She's pretty and really nice and rocks an awesome style.

I pick out another pair. "How about these?"

"She's more . . ." Nash scans the earrings. "Like this." He lifts a pair of dangly ones off the rack.

"Oh. She's complicated."

"Yeah." Nash smiles. "Exactly."

"So . . . you like complicated?"

"Apparently." Nash drills me with his intense eyes. But in a good way. In this way that's like, *You know what I mean. You were there.* And I know he's thinking that I'm complicated.

Not that he still likes me. Because if he did, then why would he be going out with Rachel? And how could I not have known they were going out?

When I get home, Dad's like, "Hey, kid. How was work?"

"A real thrill."

"That good, huh?"

"Better, even." I know that I shouldn't take out my bad mood on

Dad. But when I get like this, no one who dares to approach me is safe.

"Mom's working late," Dad says.

"Again?" It's like the third time this week.

"What do you think about breakfast for dinner?"

"I'm not hungry."

"You have to eat."

"I'll eat later."

"But I'm about to whip up some excellent frozen waffles."

"That's okay."

See, here's an example of when I get anxious about something totally random and it ruins everything. Why do I have to get all twarked up over Nash going out with Rachel, when who even cares if they're going out?

21

When I shot my first roll of film and Mom took it to get developed, she had no idea what she'd be getting back.

My photos were good. Like, *really* good.

I know that sounds conceited, but it's not. I'm just saying. Everyone loves my photos. The yearbook and newspaper editors even tried to recruit me, except I like doing my own thing. Which kind of goes against how I'm trying to be more social, but I can't compromise my art. I'm all about taking pictures that have a certain edge to them, and taking lame shots of cheesy pep rallies isn't exactly the most profound.

Sometimes it's hard to get the right exposure on a print I'm doing. I like taking what's on the film and then manipulating it so the image looks lighter or darker than it actually was. And then other times, I want to print the photo to reflect exactly how things were when I took it. Capturing the Now so I'll never forget these parts of my life.

It's so cool that I have my own darkroom. I love it in here. I'm trying to develop a photo of my dad I took when he was working out back. I shot about half a roll of him making this bookcase for my room last week. He's still not done, but I'm totally psyched. It's going to be an amazing bookcase.

The print peers up at me through its clear stop bath. I can already tell that it's not coming out right. I lightly poke the edges of the photo paper with my plastic tongs. Then I carefully clamp the edge and pick it up, moving it to the fixer.

There's this one photo I saw when I dug that box out of my parents' closet. It was another one of my dad from a few years ago, making a bookcase for a client. It would be cool to put these together somehow, then and now, transcending time.

I move the print to the wash and hang it up to dry. Then I run upstairs to their closet. I look for the box where I found it before, but it's not there. Then I find it on my dad's side of the closet.

Which is almost empty.

Okay. This is weird. Something was off before. It definitely felt emptier in here, but it wasn't like anything was exactly missing. That I noticed, anyway.

Now things are definitely missing.

Like most of his clothes. And shoes. And when I inspect the top shelf where the luggage usually is, his big suitcase is gone.

I run over to his dresser and pull open the top drawer. Empty.

The second drawer only has a few pairs of socks left. Then I go into my parents' bathroom and yank open the medicine cabinet. One whole shelf is empty. I try to think what should still be here that Dad would need every day. Like his toothbrush and razor and shaving cream. I can't find any of those things.

What the hell is going on?

It's not like he's traveling anywhere. If he was, he would have told me about it. Why would he just leave while I was at school without saying anything?

I run downstairs and find Mom at her desk, doing bills.

"Where's Dad's stuff?" I say.

She glances at me. Then she goes back to the bills. "What stuff?"

"His side of the closet's almost empty. And his suitcase is gone."

Mom puts her pen down. She doesn't say anything.

"Did he go somewhere?" I ask.

"Sort of," Mom says.

"What do you mean?"

"Why don't you sit—"

"I don't want to sit." My heart's hammering really hard and I feel dizzy. I can already tell that I don't want to know what she's going to say.

Mom looks at me. "Your dad's been staying at a friend's house."

"Since when?"

"For about a month."

"A *month*?"

"About, yes."

"But that's impossible. He's here every day. And we always have dinner together—he made us pancakes last night!"

"I know. But he sleeps at his friend's."

"Why?"

"We're not getting along."

"*What?*" That can't be right. It doesn't make any sense. My parents get along better than any other parents I know. I've never even seen them fight. I mean, they might have little disagreements here and there, but they've never had one of those scary fights with lots of screaming and throwing stuff. "Since when?"

"For a while now."

"How long's a while?"

"Marisa," Mom says as she gets up. "Things haven't been right between us since last year."

I shake my head. "No," I say. "There's no way."

"We didn't want to tell you and Sandra until we were sure."

"About what?"

"About the separation."

There's something weird going on with my hearing. The whole time Mom's explaining about how Dad is going to move out, it sounds like I'm underwater. All of her words are making this sloshing sound and I can't really grasp what she's saying.

"Why are you guys doing this?" I go.

"We have to take some time apart."

"Why?"

"To figure out what we want."

What they *want*? Don't they want to be together? Isn't that the point of getting married? "What does that mean?"

"We're not happy anymore."

"But you look happy," I say. Then I remember my birthday dinner. And how Mom pulled her hand away when Dad tried to touch her. How they didn't laugh once all night. And how tense Thanksgiving was.

"We didn't want to upset you."

Maybe it's just me, but I'm not getting this. Two people who've looked happy my whole life aren't actually happy and I had no idea? I live here. You'd think I would have a clue by now. And what's up with the whole "We're not happy anymore" line? Something like that doesn't just happen for no reason.

"But *why* aren't you happy?"

"These things happen sometimes."

"But what's the reason?"

Then Mom says something she's never said before. "I can't tell you."

"Why not?"

"It's private."

Private? *Private?* Since when is anything ever private around here? Mom's always told me everything. Well. Apparently, not everything.

"Why?" I go. There's no way I'm letting her get away with such a BS reason.

"Some things in a relationship are . . . they need to stay between the people involved. And I'm sorry you had to find out this way. Your dad wanted to tell you right away, but—"

"Tell me what?"

"About the separation," Mom says. But I don't think that's what she meant. I think she was going to say that Dad wanted to tell me the reason they're breaking up.

Because he's the reason.

And then it hits me. My dad is having an affair.

I remember when I was bringing in the mail a few weeks ago. There was a blue envelope addressed to my dad. It didn't have a return address, but the handwriting was definitely a woman's.

Oh my god. I can't believe my life is such a cliché now. I'm just like all those other kids with miserable parents.

This wasn't supposed to happen to me.

It's obvious who this "friend" Dad's staying with really is. That's why Mom doesn't want to tell me. She must be really embarrassed. Imagine being married to someone who cheated on you. Imagine that you had kids with him.

I hate my dad for doing this.

"Just tell me this one thing," I try. "There's someone else involved, right? That's part of the reason you're . . . separating?"

Mom looks scared. She obviously doesn't want to admit it. But if she gives me this piece of information, I'll stop asking about it. Which is exactly what she wants.

She nods.

So I'm right.

I hate my dad.

I'm going crazy. I am in desperate need of a distraction. All I can do is go to my room and try not to scream. I don't even know how I can wait for Dirk to come on. But somehow the hours pass and when he finally does, it's like I can vent all of my pain and anger through him somehow. He's the only person who can make me feel better no matter what. I'm instantly calmer the second his show starts.

He reads a few e-mails. I lose myself in other people's problems.

"'Dear Dirty Dirk. My parents suck. They never let me do anything and if I get below a B on a test, they totally freak. I feel like I'm going to snap and have a nervous breakdown or something and end up in a mental hospital. I can't take it anymore, but I can't talk to them. Please help. Signed, Mad Angry.'

"Oh, hey, I hear you on the lacking parental unit. I think we all do. Seriously, does anyone have parents who know what they're talking about? Or even know how to talk to us like we're real people? It's pretty obvious that our friend Mad Angry has been let down by the people who are supposed to be her role models. I'm sad to say I'm a member of that club. It never ceases to amaze me how screwed up our parents are, but then they expect us to know how to act. Last time I checked, they were the people who were supposed to be setting an example."

This is so weird. It's like everything Dirk is saying and the e-mails he's picking to read are all about my life. And the sad thing? Is that he's the only person who completely gets me right now and I don't even know who he is.

22

I get almost zero sleep that night. Sometime around five in the morning I must have fallen asleep, because when my alarm goes off I jerk awake. It takes me forever to get out of bed and I don't have time for breakfast, so I grab a yogurt to eat at the bus stop. Which is not exactly the most brilliant idea, because then I'm standing out in the cold with the brutal wind whipping my face, trying to keep the yogurt on my spoon from either freezing or flying off.

All I want to do is get to art and lose myself in making something pretty. But of course today is the one day I can't do that.

The second I get there, Mr. Goode starts yelling about how some junior lost this really important project for a state contest that's due over Christmas break. And he's panicking that we're never going to find it because this room is a disaster area and tomorrow's the last day before break. So we all have to look for it, which means cleaning up a massive mess. Mr. Goode isn't exactly known for his neatness factor. We all have these big envelopes we use to store our projects, so we're going through everything in them in case the project got shoved into one of them by mistake. Everyone's checking the drying racks and digging behind random piles of stuff and searching behind old paint containers and it's a total frenzy. The last thing I'm expecting is for Derek to talk to me.

But then he comes up to me and he's like, "So. Are you around over break?"

"Um—"

"Or are you leaving town?"

"No. I'll be here."

And then he goes, "Me, too. Maybe we should hang out."

I drop a jar of rubber cement. It doesn't break.

Derek laughs. "Is that a yes?"

"Yes!" I burst out. "I mean, yeah, sure, that sounds good."

So it's official. We finally have a date.

It's amazing how much your life can improve in only a few minutes.

I can't wait to tell Sterling. I catch her at her locker after art and I'm all, "Derek just asked me out!"

"Shut up!"

"He just came right up to me in art and asked me out!"

"That's awesome. See, I knew he liked you!"

"I was starting to wonder."

"When's the hot date?"

"Over break." I just want to be happy about Derek and get excited about our date. But can I just do that like a normal person?

No. I have to be all worried about my parents, and I'm so angry at my dad. I want to tell Sterling about the separation, but I can't. If I say it, then it's real. And there's no way I'm talking to Sandra about it. She doesn't know yet and Dad should be the one to tell her.

When I keep the bad stuff in, it only leads to worse stuff happening later. But I'm just not ready to talk about it.

"Someone's going to ask me out, too," Sterling says.

"Seriously? Who?"

"Ken."

There's no Ken in our grade.

"Ken who?" I go.

"He doesn't go here. We've been talking."

"Wait, is he Ricky's friend?"

"No. We met online."

Here's the thing. Meeting someone online? Isn't actually meeting. I never get why some girls are all carried away with "meeting" guys online when those people could be anyone.

I'm like, "Since when are you talking to guys online?"

"Since now. You have no *idea* how cute Ken is. I'll e-mail you his pic."

"So . . . he might ask you out?"

"Totally. He already said that he wants to meet me in person."

"Wow."

"He's *so* cute."

"That's . . . that's great." I think the whole thing is a big pile of really bad idea, but she's so happy and there's no way I'm ruining it for her. She's happy the way I wish I could be right now.

23

I hate that Dad found an apartment and he's moving all his stuff into it. I hate that I don't know how to fix this. And I especially hate that I can't be happy about Derek, after all this time waiting for him to ask me out.

I don't even care that Christmas is in two days. Merry freaking hoo-ha.

Even though I hate my dad right now, I'm secretly hoping that my parents will get back together. Because the thing is, I used to love him. Like, really love him, as much as you can love a dad. He was a great dad. I totally want to throw up every time I think about how he betrayed us, but under that, buried down deep in a place I don't want to admit is real, there's a tiny glimmer of hope.

Except for art and Derek, school is a total nightmare. If our break wasn't starting tomorrow, I don't think I'd be able to survive. I shuffle to global, where there's a disturbing revelation. Darius didn't do his homework.

That can't be right.

Ms. Maynard agrees. She's like, "Okay, Darius, very funny."

But Darius is like, "No. I'm serious. I didn't do it."

You could hear a cricket chirp. I mean, you know, if it were nighttime. And we were outside and all.

Ms. Maynard decides to leave that one alone.

"Okay!" She claps her hands in what's supposed to be an efficient gesture, but instead comes off as nervous. "Let's move on."

I watch Darius. He's definitely changed. I mean, other than what he's wearing. When he raises his hand to answer questions, he's not as hyper about it. He's severely toned down.

All day this anger builds up inside of me. And I'm seeing all of these things I never noticed before. It's like I have this razor-sharp awareness of how people really are. What they're really thinking when they're supposed to be paying attention in class. The things they're not saying but wish they were.

Or maybe I'm just projecting.

I don't talk to anyone for the rest of the day. Sterling keeps asking what's wrong every time she sees me, but I just say I'm PMSing. I can tell she's worried because she knows that one little thing can send me into a depression for days. And I should be psyched that I'm finally going out with Derek.

When I see Nash in the hall, I get this overwhelming urge to talk to him. But then Rachel appears and he's totally gone.

It's not unbearably cold out so I walk home from school. Exercise is supposed to help keep me stable. My therapist said how exercise releases endorphins, which make you feel good. But I'm clearly grasping at straws.

The first thing I do when I get home is take my violin into the bathroom and slam the door. We had the winter concert right before I found out about Dad and there's already stuff to practice for the spring concert. I wish I could go back to when I didn't have to know the truth about my parents. I liked my role model version of them better.

I lock myself in with a resounding click. I tighten my bow too tightly. I grind my bow with rosin so hard there's this huge cloud of dust. I sneeze. Some bow hairs snap off and peel away slowly, like they're afraid of what I'll do next. Which makes me even angrier. This is a new bow.

Why does every little thing have to be this huge challenge?

I whale on the violin. I don't even care that the notes are coming out too sharp. I'm dangerously close to tearing off the D string just from my angry vibes.

There's banging on the bathroom door. I ignore it.

Sandra won't be ignored.

"Can you *please* chill?" she yells. She rattles the doorknob. "Let me in!"

I grind harder. The notes don't even sound like notes anymore.

"Can you *shut up*?" Sandra yells.

There's no way she's leaving me alone, so I unlock the door. I open it a crack and say, "May I help you?"

"You can stop beasting on your violin. Some people are trying to read."

"And would any of those people be an annoying little nugget?" Sandra just put up this PETA poster in her room of fluffy chicks that says WE ARE NOT NUGGETS! PLEASE DON'T EAT US. I've been teasing her about it. She hates it when I call her a nugget.

She's all, "Well, at least I'm not a corroded snothead."

"It's a lot better than being a crispy little nugget."

"*Mom!*" Sandra yells. "Marisa won't get out of the bathroom!"

"Yell all you want. She's not home." What am I doing? Alienating people I have to live with? Picking some stupid fight with my little sister like I'm twelve? Destroying my expensive violin? "Sandy—"

"My *name*. Is Sandra."

"Really? I thought it was Nugget."

"You're a reject, you know that?" Sandra slams the door.

Yeah. I'm beginning to realize that I still am. But thanks for the confirmation.

24

I set my alarm for extra early this morning, even though I totally didn't need to. I couldn't sleep all night. I'm so excited that my stomach is a permanent jiggle-jaggle of nerves.

There they go again.

Jiggle.

Jaggle.

I'm a mess.

And the craziest thing? Is that I woke up super early and I'm still not ready yet. Everything I try on looks stupid and wrong. What do you wear for a day of hanging out at the Notch and seeing a movie after? I finally decide on my fave jeans and this sheer top that's both flowy and fitted that I got for Christmas. I wonder if Derek will think it's sexy. Or do boys even notice these things?

Christmas in two places was bogus. There was our usual Christmas with the tree and presents and everything, but no Dad.

We went to his new apartment for Christmas Eve and it kind of freaked me out. Sandra was freaked out, too. After my fight with Mom, she finally told Sandra about the separation. I don't think I'll ever get used to Dad not living with us. I could tell that he put a lot of effort into making everything look as nice as possible with boxes still unpacked and hardly any furniture, but it felt really staged. And of course I'm still mad at him, so the whole thing was seriously lame. I'm so mad I can't even talk to him about it. He tried talking to me, but I just left the room. I don't know why he bothered to have us over. He must feel really guilty.

But now that pathetic attempt at a holiday is in the past. And I'm determined to improve my life. Sterling and I made that reinvention pact for a reason. I can still do this.

When Derek rings my bell, the jiggle-jaggle acts up. I can't calm down. I could not be more nervous and excited and nauseous all at the same time.

As I clomp down the stairs in my new boots, a horrible thought occurs to me. I stop clomping. What if he's not as excited to see me as I am to see him? What if I look like a huge dork, opening the door with this expression like he's the best thing that's ever happened to me while his eyes glaze over with indifference?

Sandra beats me to the door.

"Are you Derek?" she goes.

"Yeah. You're Sandra, right?"

She just looks at him. I know how she feels. The shock of having a potential boyfriend pick me up for an actual date blows my mind, too.

I walk over on shaky legs.

"Hey," Derek says.

"Hi." My face feels like it's going to crack in two from my stretchy smile.

And guess what? Derek has the same smile.

Sandra rolls her eyes.

A few kids from school are at the Notch. This rocks. I want the whole school to see us together. So when we go back after break, everyone will already know that we're a couple.

Derek's like, "So . . . what do you want to do first?"

"I don't know."

"Feel like ice cream?"

"It's, like, three degrees out."

"That's why getting ice cream would be badass."

Derek is awesome.

Shake Shack is our best option for ice cream. There's a section of the counter where you can get sundaes and cones and stuff, but of course we're the only ones standing there. And the guy working the ice-cream section is on his cell phone.

We wait for him to get off.

He doesn't get off.

"Hi," Derek says. "Can we have—"

But ice-cream guy holds his hand up for us to wait.

I lean over to Derek and whisper, "Can't you see he's on a very important call?"

"And he's never getting off!" Derek whispers back.

We wait some more.

Derek goes, "This is getting ridiculous."

"Maybe he forgot we're here."

"What could he possibly be talking about that's more important than us?"

Ice-cream guy looks over at us and goes, "Help you?" He's still on the phone.

We tell him what we want.

"My treat," I tell Derek. I take out my wallet and get some singles.

"Absolutely not," he says. He stuffs the singles back in my wallet.

"But this was such a good idea." I take the singles out again.

"But it was *my* idea." He stuffs the singles back in.

"Okay. Thanks."

Ice-cream guy hands us our cones. The ice cream on mine is all crooked. It's sloping dangerously to one side.

But he's still on the phone. So I hold up my cone to show him, tilting it to balance the slanting ice-cream tower, thinking he'll make me another cone. And what does he do? He just pulls some napkins out of the dispenser and holds them out for me, still jabbering away, barely noticing the problem of the leaning ice cream, which will be impossible to eat without an inevitable major catastrophe.

"Helpful," Derek decides.

"Isn't he?"

"Let's sit over there."

It's one thing to imagine how your life would be if you had the boyfriend you've always wanted. It's a whole other thing to actually have him. I'm so excited and nervous that it's hard to eat my ice cream. I can barely follow what Derek's talking about.

Derek crunches into his cone. My ice cream is dripping.

"Here," he says. "Let me help you with that." Derek grabs my cone. He takes a huge bite of ice cream.

"Hey!"

"I'm sorry. Did you want that?"

"How can you bite into ice cream like that?"

"Like what?"

"Like with your teeth?"

"Should I be biting some other way? Man, I'm so out of it."

"No!" How does he make everything so funny? "I can't bite into anything that cold. My teeth are really sensitive. It would kill."

"Isn't there some special toothpaste for that?"

"I already use it. It doesn't help that much, though." I lick more ice cream. "Doesn't it hurt? When you bite into ice cream like that?"

"No. I have teeth of steel."

"I've heard about you. Weren't you featured on *Humans with Amazing Capabilities*?"

"Is that a real show?"

"What do you think?"

"I think you're trying to be funny."

"Oh! *Trying* to be?"

"It's okay. We can work on that."

All signs point to Derek becoming my boyfriend. And Aunt Katie says that communication is the key to having a good relationship. Which I totally get. But does that mean you have to tell the person everything about yourself? Because there's no way I'm telling Derek about my anxiety disorder. Everyone just assumed I was a freak last year. No one knows the real reason I was being so weird, and I intend to keep it that way. Anyway, it's not important for Derek to know because I'm determined to remain stable, so why freak him out over nothing? I just want to live in the Now and not worry about the rest.

Okay. If I were being really honest with myself? Then I would admit that I don't want him to know how messed up I am. I don't want him to know about my emotional problems or my parents or anything that even remotely sucks. Because if he knows how complicated I am, he might not like me anymore.

Does that count as trying to be someone I'm not?

Right when I finish my ice cream, Nash comes in with Rachel.

I don't know what to do. Should I just be myself? Or should I make an effort to go over there and say hi? And why doesn't going over there and saying hi feel like being myself?

Nash sees me looking at him and waves. I wave back.

Derek turns around to see who I'm waving to. "You're friends with Nash, right?" he goes.

"Yeah. We're friends."

"I've seen you guys around."

Then Nash and Rachel come over. It's so weird to see her like this. Rachel's always been just this girl in my classes and now she's suddenly Nash's girlfriend. It's bizarre.

Everyone says hey.

"You know Derek, right?" I ask Nash.

"Hey, man," Derek says, putting out his fist.

Nash isn't really the type of boy who goes around pounding fists. But he pulls it off and goes, "Didn't we have language arts together in seventh grade?"

Derek's like, "Did we? I can't remember that far back."

"I think so," Nash says.

We're all awkward and subtexty and I'm not even sure why. I guess the four of us hanging out together wouldn't exactly be the best combination. And not just because Nash has a ten thirty curfew, even on weekends. So I'm relieved when Nash and Rachel get fries to go.

Derek's looking at me.

"What?" I say.

He keeps looking at my mouth.

"What?" I pull a napkin out of the dispenser and wipe my mouth. "Do I have something on my face?"

"You have . . ." He leans in closer. ". . . amazing lips." And then he's kissing me. And I'm kissing him back. Right here in the middle of Shake Shack where everyone can see!

I never thought my first real kiss would be so public. But it doesn't even matter. When I'm with Derek, it's like we're the only ones who exist. Everything else just fades into the background.

25

Sterling's in a pissy mood. That Ken guy she was talking to online blocked her. He did it on New Year's Eve, which was totally lame. I was hoping that Derek would ask me to this big party on New Year's Eve, but he was at his uncle's house in New Jersey. So Sterling and I had a pathetic time, eating too many pigs in a blanket appetizers and watching people freezing their butts off in Times Square. Plus, the appetizers were the frozen kind. She didn't even have the energy to cook. We tried listening to Dirk, but he wasn't on.

Going back to school today would have been a total drag if it wasn't for Derek. And Derek kissing me in Shake Shack. And kissing me some more when he took me home. I should be feeling incredible, but every time I think about my parents my heart sinks. This might be a good time to tell Sterling about that. Everyone knows misery loves company. And keeping this kind of stuff in is seriously destructive. It's killing me, not talking about it.

Sterling keeps banging her pans around. I came over after school because I didn't want her to be alone.

"How can such a little person make so much noise?" I wonder.

"Like this." *Bang bop bang* go the pans.

"Impressive. How about using words?"

"That's so overrated."

"Fine, but I'm here to listen if you change your mind."

Sterling glances at me. For a second it looks like she's going to rant about Ken some more. But then she turns back to the chopping board.

I'm like, "Should you really be chopping those peppers in your condition?"

"Yes."

"Oh. Well . . . I sort of have to tell you something."

"I'm listening."

"No, it's . . . It's serious."

Sterling puts the knife down and sits at the counter across from me. "Okay."

How do you say something like this? Do you, like, lead up to it and explain how things got this bad? Or do you just suddenly announce how bad everything is?

I say, "My parents are separated."

Everything with Sterling changes. The anger disappears from her face. Her mouth hangs open.

"Oh my god," she says. "Since when?"

"Um. Now, I guess."

"I'm so sorry."

"Thanks."

I hate putting other people in this type of situation. Not that I've ever had to tell anyone something this heinous before. But when you tell someone something like this, it really puts them on the spot. It's like you're expecting them to say the right thing or somehow make you feel better. But of course there's nothing they can say. And there's nothing they can do.

Unless you're Sterling.

"Forget this salad," she says. She takes the chopping board and shoves it on a side counter. "There's only one solution to a problem like this." She starts mixing dough for chocolate chip cookies and whipping up her signature frappes. That's the thing about Sterling. If you're in pain, she'll put her issues aside and help you. She has strength like that.

I help by picking out what type of chocolate chips I want for the cookies.

"Comfort food is always the answer," Sterling promises. She makes the best. If you want mashed potatoes or mac and cheese, Sterling is your girl. It reminds me of when I had my retainer and all I could eat was soft food.

"I shouldn't have stopped wearing my retainer," I say.

"Random. But, okay, explain."

"Because now my tooth is crooked."

"Then why did you stop wearing your retainer?"

"It was killing me. And I kept throwing it out with my lunch. Then I'd have to dig through the garbage and everyone would be watching. It was so humiliating."

My dad was the one I told about my retainer. I knew Mom would get mad that I didn't want to wear it anymore, so I went to him instead. He told me that everything would be okay. That I shouldn't be living in pain. And he said he'd talk to Mom for me. Which I guess worked, because she never even asked me about it.

That was back when I could trust him. I thought it would always be that way between us. Where I could tell Dad anything and it would be okay. But he wasn't who I thought he was. He was this other person who was keeping secrets and living another life, going through the motions.

How could something that felt so right actually be so wrong?

26

I'm on my bed reading *The Pact* for the third time when I think I hear my dad's voice downstairs. But that can't be right. He's only been here once since I found out about the separation and that was to take Sandra out. Actually, he came to get both of us, but I said I didn't feel well. He doesn't get to come over and try to see me like he didn't just destroy our entire family. My parents have always told us that actions have consequences. Why does he think that doesn't apply to him?

This sucks. I should be high on euphoria from my first date with Derek. And going out with him again later this week. And I am, in a way. But then in this other way, all my family drama is making me feel sick.

It's exhausting.

As if all this doesn't suck enough, it's freezing in here. I need another blanket, so I go out to the hall closet for the really heavy wool one. I can hear my parents talking downstairs.

"You can try it," Mom is saying, "but I don't think she'll go for that."

"How else is this supposed to work?"

"Maybe you should have thought of that before."

Whatever Dad says next is all muffled, but he sounds annoyed. Like he has any right to be. I heard what Mom just said and I know what she meant. He should have thought about us before. As in, before he cheated on her and destroyed our lives.

I take the blanket back to my room and get under it on my bed. It's scratchier than I remember. I just want to read and forget about everything else. But that's impossible. Because someone is knocking on my door.

"Who is it?" I go.

A pause. "It's Dad."

"I don't feel like talking."

"Marisa. Open the door."

"I'm busy."

"I have something for you."

I *so* don't want to see him. Or talk to him.

"No, thanks," I say.

Another pause. Then: "I'm leaving it out here."

I wait for him to leave. Then I wait some more.

When I open my door a few minutes later, my new bookcase is sitting there. With a big, red bow on top.

He still loves me.

I run downstairs. Maybe he hasn't left yet. I run out onto the front porch. His car is still in the driveway. So where is he?

I have to talk to him. I have to know the truth. It's too hard not being able to tell him things, to feel his support, to have him in my life the way he was before.

Because I know Dad, I know that the only place he could be right now is out on the dock. And that's where I find him. I can tell by the way he's standing, leaning against the railing and looking down into the water, that he's crushed. And I'm the one who's crushed him.

"Hey, kid," Dad goes.

I lean against the railing next to him.

"It was wrong not to tell you," he says. "I wanted to tell you before I moved out."

"Then why didn't you?"

Dad shakes his head. "I had to consider your mom's feelings."

All of the rage boils up again. I go, "How could you do this to us?"

"It was the only way. We can't be separated and living in the same house."

"And whose fault is that, I wonder?"

"Don't be mad at her."

Yeah, right. Like I'm not going to hate Dad's girlfriend.

I'm like, "She wrote you a letter a while ago, didn't she?"

"Who?"

"The person I'm not supposed to be mad at."

"I was talking about your mom. Not to be mad at your mom."

"Why would I be mad at her?"

Dad scoffs. "She didn't tell you?"

"No. I guess she thought you should be the one to do that."

"Why would I—who do you think that letter was from?"

I try to say, *The woman you're having an affair with.* But I can't make those words come out.

"Is that why you've been so mad at me?" Dad says. "You think I'm having an affair?"

"You're not?"

"No! I can't believe—no. I'm not. I would never do something like that."

"Then why are you guys separated?"

"Didn't your mom talk to you about this?"

"No. She's not telling me anything."

Dad rubs his hands over his face. "I can't believe this."

"Can you just tell me? I mean . . . if you're not having an affair, then whatever it is—"

"It was her!" Dad bursts out. "Your mother's the one who's having an affair."

Oh. My. God.

"I'm sorry," Dad says. "I didn't mean for it to come out like that. I'm—" He bends over the railing. The vein on his temple is pulsing, the way it always does when he's angry.

"I can't believe I thought you . . . I'm so sorry, Dad."

"You didn't know."

Mom was the one. Not Dad. Unbelievable.

How could she let me think it was him? How could she do this to Dad?

"Hey," Dad says. "You okay?"

"No. I'm definitely *not* okay." I stomp away from the railing. "I can't believe Mom did this. I hate her!"

"Marisa—"

"How is that—" I'm so furious I can't even get the words together. I hate being so angry. And talking about it will just make me angrier. So I go, "Could we not talk about this now?"

It doesn't look like Dad's going to let me get away with my usual avoidance tactics. But then he goes, "What else has been going on in your life?"

We stay out on the dock for a long time, catching up on all the things that happened while I refused to see him. It feels good to have someone listen, even if I can't talk about everything I should. It's just good to know he's still here.

27

Being back at school as Derek's girlfriend is awesome. People are definitely noticing me more, and not in a bad way. All I want to do is be with him. The thing is, I can't tell him about my parents. Talking about it with Sterling helped and I really want to tell Nash, but Derek is out-of-bounds. Who would want to go out with a loser who's nothing but problems and misery?

When I'm with Derek, it's like none of that stuff exists. I can escape into this happy place and block out my problems. I can pretend that everything's okay. Kind of like when I'm in my dark-room.

There's a whole new series of river photos I'm developing. I've been capturing the Now of the river in each season. So far, I like the ones from last summer the best. On the sunniest days, the river has all these bright sparkles in it. The light radiates in a way that makes it seem like it's coming from within the water instead of just being reflected from the surface.

I hang up the prints to dry and head to the kitchen for a drink. I stop outside the doorway. Aunt Katie is here, talking to Mom. Mom tried to talk to me after I found out the truth from Dad, but I just went to my room and slammed the door. That was two days ago and I've been avoiding her ever since. Oh, and I found out who that blue letter was from, the one for Dad. It was from Megan, who was his high school sweetheart. She got in touch with him before the separation and he didn't even respond until he moved out. Being reunited after all these years must be weird. I wonder if you can really be just friends with someone you used to love.

There are some crumpled tissues on the kitchen table and Mom looks like she's been crying. They haven't seen me, so I move to the side where I can listen.

"You did the right thing," Aunt Katie is saying.

"Maybe," Mom says. "But that doesn't make it better."

"It'll get better. Give it time."

"I should have seen this coming," Mom says. "I shouldn't have let it get this bad. I was going to tell Marisa back in November, but . . ."

Someone's spoon clinks against a mug. They usually sit in the kitchen and drink coffee and talk about stuff, but I never knew they talked about this. Not here, anyway.

"You have to tell them now," Aunt Katie says.

"I know. I have no idea how I've avoided it this long. I hinted at it when I told Marisa about the separation, but I just couldn't admit everything."

"What are you afraid of?"

"They'll hate me. Look how Marisa's been treating me."

"She doesn't hate you. They'll understand."

"What if they don't? What will I tell Jack?"

Jack? Who's *Jack*?

"Don't worry," Aunt Katie says. "It'll work out."

"He really wants to get to know them . . . and I hate the girls not knowing about him. . . . I just wish I knew how to do this."

"It's not like Mom gave us much to go by." They laugh for some private reason.

Who the hell is Jack? We don't know any Jack. And the only way Mom would meet someone new would be at work, where—

Wait. Jack who came to dinner Jack? How could she like that guy? He was a total dumbass!

"This kind of stuff happens a lot these days," Aunt Katie says. "Separation, divorce, stepparents . . . it's very common."

"God. What does that say about us?"

"That you're not settling. That you're insisting on happiness."

"I feel so selfish."

"Don't. Jack gives you what you need. There's no way you knew this would happen when you got married."

"It was a good marriage." Mom's voice cracks. "We had nineteen good years."

"And that's what's important."

Suddenly, I'm standing in the kitchen.

"Hi, hon," Aunt Katie says to me. She darts a glance at Mom. "How did the pictures turn out?"

I stare at Mom. Ever since I found out that she was the one

who destroyed us, she's seemed like a whole different person. All this time . . . how could I not have known?

"You should have told me!" I yell. All this rage is boiling up. It's the kind of rage you can't let go of. It boils up inside of you and when something like this happens, it explodes.

"I should go," Aunt Katie says.

"No," I tell her. "Stay. Stay and hear how my mother let me think it was all Dad's fault and never told me the truth."

Mom tries to say something else, but I don't let her. "No! You let me believe it was Dad! You said someone else was involved and that's why you guys separated! You should have told me it was your fault!"

"It wasn't—"

"You wrecked our family for some other guy? Seriously? You're *married*!"

"Jack and I—"

"I don't want to hear it!" I scream. I run up to my room and slam the door. Then I open it and slam it again, louder.

This is not real.

Except it is.

I wish I could tell Derek all of this. And I wish things with Nash were the way they used to be. We started talking more after I saw him in Shake Shack. I don't know if he'll ever feel comfortable around me again, but it seems like he's trying.

My computer dings and an IM box pops up. It's Nash. Like he could tell what I was just thinking.

dorkbot10013: Are you there?

f-stop: wishing i were anywhere but.

dorkbot10013: Sounds fun. How's that chem homework going?

f-stop: my brain refuses to do my homework for me.

dorkbot10013: You should get a brain refund. Or hey, I hear
they're on sale this week at Target.

f-stop: wait, they sell brains?

dorkbot10013: You didn't know?!

f-stop: i'll pass. i'm a lost cause anyway.

dorkbot10013: I think not. Everyone hates homework.

f-stop: no, this is bigger than that. everything's messed up.

dorkbot10013: Like what?

f-stop: like my parents.

dorkbot10013: Are they fighting?

f-stop: it's more than that.

dorkbot10013: I'm calling you.

When my cell rings, I'm relieved. I can finally tell Nash everything. I have a feeling that he'll find a way to make me feel better.

I tell him about the separation and everything my dad said and
the fight I just had with my mom.

Nash goes, "I can relate."

"Really?"

"My mom ditched us when I was eleven."

I knew Nash only lived with his dad, but I've never asked him
where his mom is. I learned to mind my own business the hard
way. I was friends with this girl in middle school who only lived

with her mom. When I asked where her dad was, she told me he
was in rehab. I stopped asking after that.

But Nash was the one who brought it up. So I ask, "Why did
she leave?"

"I don't know exactly. She just said, 'I can't do this anymore.'
And the next day she was gone."

"That's just like what my dad did. Only, he didn't tell me anything."

"I hate that you're going through this," Nash says.

"It's so unfair. My parents were like the only ones who weren't
killing each other. They didn't even fight!"

"I have an idea. Can you come over?"

"When?"

"In like, half an hour?"

"I'll be there." I could *not* get out of here fast enough.

"When my mom left, there was one thing that made me feel
better. I think it might work for you, too."

"What is it?"

"You'll see when you get here."

I don't know what I was expecting. But when Nash flings open
the door to his room and booms, "Ta-dah!" it wasn't this.

He's got his room set up like a private movie screening. A stack
of DVDs is on the coffee table. A big bowl of popcorn is on his
bed. And there's extra pillows for me to lean on because he knows
I love the extra pillows.

"Wow," I say. "This is impressive."

"Thank you, thank you."

"You didn't have to do all this."

"I know. But I wanted to."

Nash is into obscure and/or retro movies. I'm not so much into the obscure, but I'm definitely liking the retro. This one time when we were burned out on the longest lab write-up ever, we took a movie break. He wanted to watch this one called *Pump Up the Volume*, but I voted for *When Harry Met Sally*, which started this whole detailed critique of every eighties movie Nash had ever seen. So now he has a stack of eighties movies, some that I've heard of and some that I haven't, and watching them together is his plan. Which I think rocks.

It feels really good being friends with Nash again. I can sense something changing between us, shifting back to where it was before. And the way we're laughing and talking, it's just like we've been friends this whole time. Like he never tried to kiss me. Like I never rejected him. Just like we used to be.

*

February - April

*

28

Nash has a new shirt.

News like this would normally seem so uneventful that it wouldn't even be classified as news. But with Nash, it's a whole different story.

This is major.

Nash never has new shirts. All of his clothes look like they're from some unidentifiable time period when the things people wore just weren't cool. Oversize flannels, strange jeans, outdated sneakers, like that. He's never really cared about his clothes before. And even though he's taller than he was at the beginning of the year, everything still seems to fit. More or less. I always feel like I just want to grab him and take him to the Notch and force him to buy stuff from this decade.

His new shirt rocks.

"You have a new shirt," I notify him. We're on his bed, watching another retro movie. This one's about a slacker boy who likes the valedictorian and how they get together after graduation.

"Oh, yeah. Do you like it?"

"I love it. Where'd you get it?"

"Urban Outfitters."

"Get out."

"Yeah, I think—"

"That's not possible." There's no way Nash not only got a new shirt, but actually went to a cool store to get it. I didn't even know he knew what Urban Outfitters *was*.

"Why not?"

"When was the last time you got a new shirt?"

"Uh . . ." Nash thinks. "Like . . ." He thinks some more.

"Never mind. I've never seen you with a new shirt."

"Well, now you have."

"Apparently. So when did you get it?"

"I didn't. Rachel got it for me."

I should have known this was Rachel's influence. She's definitely having an effect on Nash. Why else would he suddenly get a fashion clue?

"It's nice," I say.

"Thanks."

"So. How are things going with you guys?"

"Great."

"You never told me you liked her. I didn't even know you were going out until you showed up that day at Claire's."

"Yeah."

"Why didn't you tell me?"

"Oh. Well . . . I guess I didn't want to jinx it. Or anything."

Nash tells me this funny story involving a Rubik's Cube from their first date and I wonder why I want to hear it but at the same time I don't. Why can't I just be happy for him? Why does everything always have to bother me so much?

I reach for the popcorn at the same time Nash does. Our hands touch in the bowl.

"When did she get you that shirt?" I go.

"Yesterday. Good thing, too, because I completely ignored my laundry."

Nash has laundry issues. With Nash and his dad, there's a lot of basic stuff they don't know. They haven't really learned how to do simple things like laundry. It's not like his mom stopped to explain it on her way out the door. I remember this one time last year when Nash threw darks and lights into the same load and all of his white shirts came out pink. Or the time he left his wet clothes in the washing machine overnight and everything smelled like mildew. That was gross.

This shirt is a total improvement over all that laundry drama.

I'm like, "Wow, so . . ."

Technically, Nash and I are friends. Which means we should be able to talk about the normal stuff that friends talk about, like who we're going out with and what we did with them.

". . . so you guys are . . ."

Only, the other stuff gets in the way. Like how I know Nash liked me as more than a friend.

"... getting serious," I conclude.

"I know."

Now that I think about it, I don't want to hear about Rachel any more than Nash probably wants to hear about Derek.

29

I once read that time doesn't really exist. It's just a concept invented by humans. And how quickly time passes depends on the way we're perceiving it. Like, when I'm making out with Derek, time accelerates to warp speed. But when I'm at work or waiting around until the next time I can see him, one second takes forever. Let's just say that time's been passing really quickly lately.

We've been spending every day we can together. All I want to do is be with him. And when I'm not with him, all I can think about is the next time I can be with him. We kiss for hours. I never thought just kissing could be so intense. But it is. So things are getting serious. Derek even told me he loved me on Valentine's Day. Of course I told him I love him back. That was four days ago and I've been ecstatic ever since.

Well, until today. Today has two versions.

Version #1. The Way Things Were Supposed to Go.

When I get to school, Derek is already waiting for me at our spot. He kisses me. Two girls walking by stare at us with longing in their eyes. We walk in and own the hall with our perfect relationship, rising above the crumbling bits of all the breakups that have happened around us.

Version #2. What Actually Happened.

When I get to school, Derek's not at our usual meeting spot on the front lawn next to the small tree. He's *always* at our spot. I wait ten minutes for him in the wicked cold. Then I go in.

This sinking, nervous feeling attacks my stomach. I think I know why Derek's not here. And where he is instead. But maybe that's just my paranoia flaring up.

Don't jump to conclusions. Think rationally based on real information.

"Hey, sexy!" Derek jogs up to me in the hall. He's wearing the new shirt I picked out for him. It's got that guy from the classic Maxell ad, sitting in a chair and being blown away by the speakers, which are blasting so hard his tie is flying out behind him. "Where you been?"

"I was waiting for you."

"I was waiting for *you!*"

"Where?"

"At our spot."

"Well, I was there and you weren't."

"Oh, did you get here early?"

I really don't want to fight. Especially over something that's probably nothing. So I'm like, "Whatev. Let's just go."

"Isn't your homeroom the other way?"

"So? I was going to walk you."

"Then you'll be late."

"No, I won't. Or you could walk me."

Derek smiles. "Then *I'll* be late." He kisses me in this way that's so divergent from the kiss in Version #1 I don't even know what to do with it.

"We can't have that, now, can we?" I say, trying to minimize the sarcasm in my voice.

"Not so much. See you later."

"Yeah," I yell after him. "Later." But he's already halfway down the hall.

I'm in a horrendous mood all day. And not just because Derek is acting weird. Finally getting to be with him is exciting and exhausting at the same time. Sometimes it feels like I'm posing for him, like I'm acting a certain way I think he wants me to be, or how I wish I was. I don't even know why I do it. I never feel totally comfortable around Derek, like I can just be myself.

In global, Ms. Maynard gives us a worksheet to do in groups. Darius is all over it. He's half done already and we just got it two minutes ago.

Darius is back. And he's on fire.

No one can touch him now. It's like he was suddenly resurrected from the flames of academic destruction when the new semester started and now he's got all this renewed energy that is full-on scary. He obviously figured out that the hard-core slackers he was hanging out with before weren't worth his time. It was so strange seeing Darius with this pack of boneheads who think it's cool to cut class and smoke and generally mess up their lives before their lives even have a chance to begin. I guess it's further evidence that people can always shock you, no matter how well you think you have them figured out.

I can see how that crowd might be appealing at first. Imagine you're Darius. Since kindergarten, you've been the overachiever, the kid who knows everything and thinks life is over if he gets an A-minus on one quiz. So after years of trying to be perfect, you're tired, right? And here are some kids who, for whatever reason, want to let you into their group when you've never really belonged to any group before. You were always the loner, the freak, the nerd who sits alone at lunch. And now here's your chance to belong. Even if it's to a loser group, it's still a group and you can still belong. If you change the way you dress. And the way you are. You just want to belong so badly and this group lets you in and you don't care if it messes you up.

Teachers had a hard time figuring that out. They kept saying what a shame it was that Darius was wrecking his life and being this badass poser they didn't recognize anymore. They never thought about what it was like to be Darius. They only cared about the image of what they wanted him to be.

Of course, his chances of getting into Harvard are slimmer now. Slacking for three months will place him below all the straight-A kids who never even take one night off from homework. But he's still hoping to get that magic letter senior year. Even when Darius was slacking, he was still doing better than most of us.

Kelvin scrunches his desk closer into the group cluster. He's new this year. All I know about him so far is that he moved here from New York and he transferred into this class from fourth-period global when his schedule got all switched around this semester.

"Put that Malcolm X was about to announce his changed attitude toward violence when he was assassinated," Kelvin tells Darius. We're doing a unit on leaders who've had a significant impact on society, both positive and negative.

"Already got it," Darius mumbles over the frantic scratching of his pencil.

"Okay, everybody!" Ms. Maynard eventually yells. "Let's go around and see what we came up with."

Kelvin's hand shoots up like a flame. Ms. Maynard calls on him.

"I think it's absurd that some dimwit who didn't even win the election was president," Kelvin starts. "How was that even allowed? I'm just in shock that it actually happened in a democratic society."

He looks around at the other kids, most of whom are gaping at him. We're not used to this much action around here.

"It actually happened!" Kelvin yells.

Everyone stares at him.

"Thank you, Kelvin," Ms. Maynard segues. "Let's hear from the other teams. Linda, what did—"

"Isn't anyone else upset about this?" Kelvin interrupts. "Doesn't anyone else *care*?"

"Yeah, we care," Darius says, trying to calm Kelvin down before he bolts out of his seat and tips Darius's notebook onto the floor, "but there's not much we could do about it. It's history."

"That," Kelvin says, "is so not true. The point of learning about history is so we can improve the future. Don't you guys know about grassroots efforts? Or national political initiatives? We can be the *change*, people!"

I feel bad for Kelvin. He's obviously used to a lot more excitement and kids who actually care about these things back in New York. The ennui is so thick around here it's like a permanent fog. It would take something major for that to change.

Derek picks me up after class. Everyone sees him waiting for me in the hall when they leave. Which is why I take a long time to get my stuff together. I want everyone to know that we're this solid couple and nothing can destroy us. And I love the anticipation of knowing he's waiting for me.

Except things are different this time. Because when I go out to the hall, there's no adoring look from Derek. There's no sarcastic comment about how much global blows. There's no planning to go out this weekend.

There's Derek talking to Sierra.

I wait for him to notice me near the door. Derek is turned away from me, but Sierra sees me watching. She moves closer to Derek and says something. He laughs at what she says.

I hate this. I want to make it stop.

But I can't. I have no power over it.

Or maybe I do.

I go over and stand next to Derek. He says, "Oh, hey, Marisa!"

"Oh," I say. "Hey."

Sierra gives me an icy stare.

"Let's go," Derek tells me.

We walk down the hall. I wait for him to tell me what that was about.

He doesn't.

I avoid talking for as long as I possibly can, giving him a chance to speak up.

He doesn't.

Then I go, "So. What were you guys talking about?"

"Yearbook."

"Oh."

I wait for more explanation. There is none.

"So are you guys . . . like . . . friends now?" I say.

"Something like that."

"What does that mean?"

"We're not—we don't hang out or anything, but we're friendly."

I wonder how friendly he means by friendly.

How can Derek be friends with her? Didn't she break up with him? So then why would he still want to associate with her? And why would she still want to talk to him?

I'm so confused.

But of course, I can't ask him this stuff. He'll find out how paranoid I am or think that I don't trust him. I should just relax. What's the big deal, anyway? He can talk to whomever he wants. They're just friends.

Except I don't want them to be friends.

Here's what I want: For Derek and Sierra to never talk again. For him to hate her now. It would make my life so much easier. Not because of Derek. He said they're just friends. But I saw Sierra's face when she was talking to him and the way she leaned in closer to him. I recognize that look. I recognize that lean.

She still likes him.

"Do you think Sierra still likes you?" I ask.

Derek laughs. "After what she did? I don't think so."

"What did she do?"

"Um, she dumped me?"

"Oh, I thought you meant something else."

"I think that makes enough of a statement that someone doesn't like you anymore, don't you?"

"Yeah," I say. Because I do. Which is why I don't get why she still likes him. The only thing I know for sure is that she does.

My heart hurts. I always assumed that heartache meant loving someone who didn't love you back or missing someone you love when they're far away. I never knew it was an actual ache in your heart.

Time for some All Talk, No Action therapy.

Tonight Dirk's making me laugh so hard I'm on the floor. Sometimes he does this segment called "Strange Human Behavior: Field Observations," where he talks about how ridiculous people can be. He makes the everyday stuff we all do so hilarious. Like how elevator rides are way more uncomfortable than they should be.

"Ever notice how no one looks at anyone else in elevators?" Dirk goes. "People will look anywhere but at each other. They get all fixated on the floor numbers like they're the most fascinating stuff in the world. Would it be so wrong to make eye contact? Why are people so scared of other people in confined spaces?

"And why do restaurants always have that sign in the bathroom saying 'employees must wash hands'? Shouldn't it say 'employees must wash hands, and so should you'? Who looks at that sign and goes, 'Hey, great, I don't work here, so I can take my gross, bacteria-infested hands back to the table without washing them and dig right in. Sweet!' I mean, do we really need a sign for that? Really?"

When I go to sleep, I'm still laughing. I'm not even thinking about Derek.

30

We just had this huge blizzard. Twenty-three inches of snow are covering the whole town. If we weren't on winter break, this would be the first snow day of the year. But of course, we are.

I'm so over winter. And I can't stop thinking about the whole Derek and Sierra thing. So I just want to hide out in my room and write on my wall.

My wall manifesto started with just a corner I hid under some sheet music I put up. But now half my wall is covered with writing. It has my own work, the best lines from books, quotes from movies, that sort of thing. I use charcoal sticks, so everything can come off. Mom went ballistic when she first saw how I was writing all over my wall. She didn't chill until I showed her how the charcoal washes right off without hurting the paint. She still hates that I write on my wall, but Dad convinced her to encourage my "creative expression."

To me, it's more like venting. When I get so bothered by something that it's all I can think about, it can take over my entire life. And even when I tell myself to stop thinking about it and try to force myself to think about something else, the something else never sticks and the original thought always finds its way back in. This can go on for days.

Like the thing with Derek and Sierra.

There's a knock on my door. I go, "Come in."

Dad's all wrapped up in his heavy winter gear. He called a while ago to say he's coming over. He still wants to do the things we normally do together. Every year on the first snow day (or, in this case, what would have been the first snow day), everyone goes to the hill for sledding. It's like the whole town shuts down and everyone comes out for the party, acting like they're ten years old again.

He's like, "Ready for the hill?"

"I don't think so."

"Hot date?"

"*Dad.*"

"Is that a no?"

"I want to write."

"Well, we're leaving now, so we'll see you out there if you change your mind."

"Who's going?"

"Just me and Sandra. See you there!"

"Maybe . . ." I just want to write. It's like once I get those obsessive thoughts out of my head, once they're written down, they're somehow set free and I can move on.

I take down a photo of me and Sterling at the beach two summers ago and move it to my bulletin board. I move a poster of Jared Leto from *My So-Called Life* that Sterling found in an old *Sassy* magazine. Then I take down diagrams with these fun psychology tests. I inspect my new space. I should have enough room for what I want to do.

My most recent wall rant was all about anticipation. How something you're looking forward to seems awesome when you imagine the way you want it to be. But then once that thing happens for real, it sucks so freaking bad. What's the point of imagining how your life should be when the reality is always such a disappointment?

I select a fat charcoal stick. In the new space, I write:

*Still hiding and
    afraid to let go.
Waiting for you to find me
    uncover me and
        show me the way.*

Time does weird things when I'm writing. It speeds up so that an hour feels like a minute. I just get into this zone of laser focus and the whole day slips away. Which is a good thing if writing's making me feel better. But all I've been doing today is hiding in my room, feeling bad. When I get into a rut like this, I'm supposed to try out new ways of behaving and reacting. Which is why I need to leave.

Sterling already IMed and Nash called to see if I'm going. So I put on my snow pants, my thickest sweater over two shirts, my big boots, and head downstairs. Dad's going to be relieved to see me on the hill.

Mom's sitting on the couch, drinking tea and reading. I've pretty much been ignoring her, and she's pretty much been letting me have my space. Of course, that can't last forever.

I sit down next to her. My snow pants crinkle.

"So you've decided to go?" Mom says.

"Yeah. Why aren't you going?" I think Mom only went to the snow day sledding event one time. She likes when no one's home and she has the house to herself. Even though all she does is read and drink tea, which she could totally do while we're here.

"This book is so good I literally cannot put it down."

"What is it?" I bend over to look at the cover.

"*Nineteen Minutes*. It's about a school shooting."

"I love Jodi Picoult!" It's kind of weird to think about my mom reading books by the same author I like.

I have a feeling that Mom wants to start up a heavy conversation that I really don't want to have, so I say bye and get out of there.

The first thing that happens when I get to the hill is a little kid almost knocks me over, racing by on his sled. It's way crowded out here. I can't find Sterling anywhere, but Nash is over by the big tree.

"Hey," Nash says. "You're here."

"I'm here."

"Welcome to the festivities. It's all very exciting. We're sitting on slabs of plastic and sliding down this big hill."

"Sounds creative."

"We're original around these parts."

"Where's Rachel?"

"She has the flu. Where's Derek?"

"He hates sledding."

"How can anyone hate sledding?"

"I know. He thinks these town events are hokey."

"Well, excuse us."

"Have you seen Sterling?"

"You just missed her. She invited some people over for hot chocolate."

"Which people?"

"Some of those French Club girls, I think."

Sterling makes the best hot chocolate. She uses three types of chocolate and always gives you extra marshmallows.

I bounce up and down in the freezing cold.

"Cold?" Nash says.

"Are you seriously asking me if I'm cold?"

"Nah, that was rhetorical."

I'm completely frozen. Even with all of my layers, the cold always finds a way to get in. I don't do winter. I simply do not care to participate. But everyone's having so much fun and I love sledding and Nash looks really happy that I showed up, so I let myself get into it.

We only have two sleds at home, and Dad took both of them

for him and Sandra. So Nash is letting me use his. We trudge up to the top of the hill, which takes forever since the snow is so high. I wrap my scarf around my face so that only my eyes are exposed. Now all I need is an eyeball warmer.

When we get to the top, Nash goes, "Do you want the front or the back?"

"Um . . . the whole thing?"

"Then where am I gonna sit?"

"Oh! I thought we were taking turns."

"Why would we do that? We can take twice as many rides if we both go."

All the other times I was out here when Nash was, he was just my neighbor who I saw at school and town events and out on the dock, this boy I used to play with a million years ago. I remember watching him pull some kids in his sled a few years ago, letting them take a bunch of rides. Now he's my friend and we're sharing his sled.

"I'll take the back," I tell him. "Less scary that way."

"Don't worry," Nash says. "I'll protect you."

We get on. I don't know where to put my legs.

"Here," Nash goes. He wraps my legs around him so my boots are pressing against the front of the sled. His legs are bent over mine with his knees pointing up near his chin.

He's like, "Ready?"

"Ready."

"Hang on!"

And we're off. This is the best hill for sledding because the slope starts out really steep, but then it becomes more gradual, so you can build up scary speed and glide for as long as you want.

The icy air whips by. It feels like we're about to tip over, so I hold on to Nash. And I don't let go until he stops the sled.

"Dude!" he says. "That was wild!"

"Totally."

"Did you want to go farther? I just thought . . . you know, since we have to walk all the way back up—"

"No, I do the same thing. The steep part is the funnest."

"Exactly."

We climb back up and sled down again so many times that my fingers are numb and my nose is running. But I don't care. I can't remember the last time I felt this alive.

31

Dirty Dirk is everywhere. I don't know how he does it. He just seems to know everything that's going on with everybody.

Maybe he has spies. He's probably one of the rich kids, so he can pay people to spy for him and report back with everyone's secrets. No one seems paranoid about being spied on, though. Everyone's loving how you can listen to Dirk almost every night and he always says just what you want to hear.

I never really thought about the way I talk before I started listening to Dirk. But now I'll be saying something in class, and I'll stop myself and think how Dirk would say it. Like how I could say it better, the way he always seems to do with the most basic things you think couldn't be said any other way.

And he knows stuff. A lot of stuff. Stuff you definitely want to hear. He's so freaking smart about human nature and the way people are. He makes these observations that answer all of the questions you have about why people act the way they do. I swear, it's like a major revelation every time you listen to his show. Or he'll talk about the exact same things that have been bothering you recently, like he's in your head somehow.

Take the other night, for example. Dad was picking me up the next morning to spend the day with me and I'd just had a huge fight with my mom. She keeps pressuring me to talk to her and meet Jack and there's just no way any of that is happening. So I was thinking about how crazy it was that I went from hating Dad and loving Mom to the other way around, and I already knew I'd be getting zero sleep. I couldn't stop fixating on how unfair it all was. But then Dirk came on and said how when the parental unit is going crazy, the best way to deal is to remove yourself from the situation immediately.

"The trick is to not get overly involved," Dirk explained. "Yeah, they're your parents and yeah, you probably have to live with at least one of them, but that doesn't mean they have to take over your life. You already have a life. Live it. Let them work out their craziness on their own."

It made so much sense, hearing it from Dirk. Just because my mom had an affair and my dad moved out doesn't mean my life is over.

Since it's almost time for All Talk, No Action to come on, I get ready. I have my Jones Fufu Berry soda and my furry lavender backrest pillow thing. I set everything up on my bed.

Some nights Dirk doesn't come on. By now, there are so many

kids listening to the show that when he doesn't come on, kids are actually bummed out the next day. But most nights he's on and you can hear everyone talking about the show the whole next day. That's because he usually exposes something or someone that deserves to be outed. He totally protects everyone else, especially the kids who are getting a raw deal.

I think the reason why so many of us love Dirk is that when he talks, it's like we're venting through him. Like we're all in this together, feeling the same frustration and pain. It's so weird how much I rely on him to get me through this freezing February and I don't even know who he is. I wish there was a way that I could tell him how much he means to me in person. But he remains a mystery. Which bothers us, because everyone loves him and wants to know him for real.

Right at the dot of eleven, music blasts from my computer speakers. He's on.

"What's good, y'all?" Dirk says. "Hope you're hanging right tonight. The communication is piling up here on All Talk, No Action, so let's get to it."

You can hear him clicking around on his keyboard. I wish I were sitting there with him, wherever he is, on the other side of the secret.

"'Hey, Dirk,'" he reads. "'I'm in love with this gorgeous boy, but I'm not sure if he likes me. I've thought about asking him out, but I don't want to be pushy. We have a class together where he's not doing so great (I saw his grade on the last paper we got back) and I'm good in that class, so I was thinking of asking him if he wants help with our next paper or something. Do you think I should tell him that I like him? Or should I just do something nice for him so he notices me? Love your show!'

"Dude. If I had a dollar for every time I got an e-mail like this I'd be one rich bastard. Living large in Aruba with my own personal hottie masseuse.

"Let me break this down for you. It's really simple, once you understand the basics. Fact: Guys are not that complicated. We're pretty simple animals. We like to sleep and eat and game. We like attention from the ladies, or from the dudes if you swing that way—it's all good. But too much attention is a turnoff. No one wants to feel crowded. Think about it like this: Does a wild animal like to be trapped in a cage? Yeah, we're tame. But we still have the same needs."

Most boys in our class don't know half this stuff. Or they might know it, but they would never admit it. But Dirk doesn't care about looking cool or protecting his ego or any of that other insanity fueled by testosterone. He's just telling it like it is. Reaching out to people who've been waiting to connect with someone who gets them.

"Listen. Guys and girls? We're different. No joke. Just because we're both types of human doesn't mean we have much else in common. Which is why, for all the ladies out there in Listening Land, tonight is your lucky night. For one night and one night only, I'm going to expose the cold, hard truth about guys. If every girl could hear how guys really are, your lives would change like that." He snaps so we can all hear how fast our lives would change.

"You'll save yourselves years of pain and torture if you know how we think. So let's break it down, shall we?

"First off, girls put way too much effort into something that's not even anything. They'll like a guy. They'll pick up on some clue that they stretch and twist until it magically means that he likes her. And then all of a sudden they're fixated on this dude who doesn't even know they exist."

Okay. How does he *know* all this? Does he have five sisters or something?

"Simplify your lives, ladies. I'll make it easy for you. I have here"—sounds of a paper being waved around—"a list of things every girl should know. And I want every girl out there to turn it up, call your friends, and pay attention. So let's give everyone out there a minute to regroup."

Something I don't recognize blasts from the speakers. I didn't realize I was so musically ignorant. I've never heard most of the songs Dirk plays.

"If you are female, this one's for you. And if you're the proud owner of additional appendages, feel free to disagree.

"How Guys Really Are, by Dirty Dirk. One. You can't convince a guy to like you. We either feel it or we don't. This is pretty self-explanatory. There's no way you can change our minds. Basically, if we like you, you'll know. And if you don't—"

My cell rings. I really don't want to pick up, but then I see that it's Sterling.

"Hey," I go.

"Are you listening?"

"Of course."

"Where was this guy when I needed him?"

"Tell me about it." I keep the phone pressed to one ear and listen to Dirk with the other.

"Two," Dirk says. "We hate big emotional talks. We will do anything to avoid any type of serious talk, especially when the talk is 'about the relationship.'

"Three. Just because a girl is feeling it all seriously on her end doesn't mean the guy wants anything more than a casual hookup. Don't assume interest means interest in anything beyond your body."

"Ouch," Sterling says. "That's harsh."

"I know."

"I know that sounds harsh," Dirk says, "but I'm giving it to you like it is. This isn't sugarcoated so it goes down easier, people. This is the brutal reality all around you and it's to your advantage to be informed."

"Can he hear us?" I ask.

"Probably. He already knows everything else."

"Four. If a girl starts out all casual with a guy and she doesn't tell him that she wants a relationship, it will never become a relationship. If you give a guy the impression that casual is okay with you, that's all he'll ever want. Be straight with him from the start. If he gets scared and runs away, he wasn't right for you."

"Totally!" Sterling yells. "It's all so basic! How could I not *know* this stuff?"

"Five. No guy wants to watch a girl cry. No guy wants to be

yelled at for being an asshole. So when girls think we're scum for dumping them or completely avoiding the breakup talk altogether, it's actually that we're preventing torture for everyone involved. We see it like this: By avoiding an emotionally traumatic confrontation, you'll feel better and so will we. Which relates to item six. When a guy is dumping a girl, all he wants to do is say 'it's over,' and then get the hell out of there. He doesn't want the girl dragging it out for three hours."

"Whoa," I say.

"Seriously."

"I'm not saying I think the way we are is right," Dirk goes. "It's actually pretty messed up. I know we're slime. But it's the way we are. So girls have two choices. They can either fight our natural tendencies, or they can go with the flow. And now you know."

Music blasts again.

"He's a freaking genius," Sterling announces.

"It's some scary stuff, but I'd rather know than not know."

"Uhhh! Why does it have to be so *complicated*?"

"Seriously."

"It's killing me. If I didn't have Paul, I don't even know."

I have no idea what to say about that. Paul is this new guy Sterling's been talking to online. She's spending so much time online these days it's like she's completely addicted. I want to be supportive and I definitely don't want to get in a fight about how some sketchy online guy is preventing her from having a real boyfriend, but I can't force myself to be okay with this. It's just wrong.

"Are you there?" Sterling asks.

"Yeah."

"You got quiet."

"No, I'm just . . . do you know who this is?"

"It's me, dude."

"No, the music."

"Oh. Yeah, I think it's the Pixies."

"Who's that? I've never even heard of them."

"It's this . . . um . . . yeah, I don't really know either."

"Who do you think Dirk is?"

"Like I haven't been trying to figure that out all year?"

"What grade do you think he's in?"

"He's probably a senior," Sterling goes. "He's way more mature than any of the chuckleheads in our grade. All I know is, this boy sounds like my ultimate fantasy."

"Take a number." I don't know anyone who doesn't listen to Dirk now. All the girls are in love and the boys like how he rats out all the evildoers.

"I can't believe no one knows who he is yet," Sterling says.

"There's got to be a way to find out."

"Yeah, but how?"

"We haven't thought of it yet. But we will."

32

I've never seen Nash this upset. He's so upset he can't even tell me what's wrong.

He came into Claire's today. He didn't even say hi or anything. He just came right up to the register and went, "What time do you get off?" His eyes were all red.

I said, "Uh . . . seven. I get off at seven."

"Good. Can I come over?"

"Okay. What's—"

"I can't talk about it now," Nash said. "See you later."

He almost smacked into the glass door when he left, like he didn't notice it was there. You could see him reach for the handle at the last second.

Nash still isn't telling me what's wrong. Which is why we're just hanging out in my room with Colin Hay playing and nobody talking. Just when I'm getting worried that Nash is having some sort of mental breakdown, he goes, "Rachel broke up with me."

"Shut up! Why?"

"She said I'm too intense."

"But intense is good! Girls like intense!"

"Not Rachel."

"How is intense a bad thing?"

"She said I get emotionally attached too soon. And she's not ready for that."

"So . . . then why can't you just take things slower?"

"I don't want to take things slower! I'm too intense, remember?"

Someone pounds on my door.

"What?" I yell.

"Your music's too loud!" Sandra yells from the hall.

"I know!" I yell back.

"Turn it down!"

I turn it down. She stomps away and slams her door.

"It's not even like I was moving that fast with anything," Nash goes. "I just really like her and I thought she liked me, so . . ."

"What did she mean by 'emotionally attached'?"

"No idea. Maybe like . . . something about how I'm too intrusive, like too interested in her life or something. But isn't that how you get when you're in a relationship?"

"Yeah," I agree. But what do I know? My relationship's technically still in that new euphoric stage where everything's supposed to be awesome. Too bad I can't figure out how to get to the awesome place.

"She likes me," Nash says. "She said she likes me."

"She obviously likes you. If she didn't like you, she wouldn't have gone out with you."

"Yeah, but she said she thought I liked her more than she liked me. And how that wasn't fair to me because I deserve to be with someone who likes me equally as much."

Oooh, that's gotta sting. That's like saying I like you, but not really. Or I like you, but there's a limit to how much. Because you suck. And if you didn't suck so bad, then maybe I'd like you more.

"I wish there was something I could do," I say.

"There is."

"Name it."

"Can I stay over tonight?"

"What?"

"I don't want to be alone."

"Isn't your dad home?"

"Exactly. That's where the 'alone' part comes in."

"Oh. Totally, of course you can. There's an air mattress in the hall closet."

This is worse than I thought. Nash must have really liked Rachel. Maybe he even loved her. And still loves her. When someone rips your heart out, there's nothing you can do to change how you feel about them. You just have to keep feeling that way until it goes away.

Unless it never does.

33

There's a sub in geometry. You have to give him credit for trying. He's attempting to give us directions for some worksheet he's passing out, but nobody's listening. Because nobody's going to finish it. Some of us won't even look at it. We all know it's just busywork that's never going to be graded, no matter what the sub tells us.

Sub in math + bogus worksheet = free time.

Except you still have to look like you're doing the work or you could get in trouble. So groups of three or four move their desks together. We huddle over our worksheets for a minute, writing our names at the top. Exhausted after this physical exertion, the gossip begins. I tune everything out. I saw Derek and Sierra in the hall again yesterday and it looked even worse than the first time I saw them talking. I was up all night replaying their flirty little interlude until I wanted to scrape the memory part of my brain right out of my head.

I need to analyze this with Sterling. So after school, I go to her locker.

"I need to talk to you," I say.

"What's up?"

"The whole Derek/Sierra thing. I can't stop thinking about it."

"Didn't we go over this last night?"

She's right. We IMed for like two hours, figuring out what I should do. Our conclusion was that I can't worry about things I have no control over. And that Derek is my boyfriend, not Sierra's. And that I have to chill. I want to be that person. The confident girlfriend person who isn't jealous or annoying and doesn't care who her boyfriend talks to.

So I got in bed and tried to relax. But it didn't work. All I could think about is if Derek and Sierra were talking those two times, how many other times have they talked without me knowing about it? And what's with all the touching? And why does Derek want to be around someone who dumped him?

Sterling slams her locker.

"Yeah," I tell her. "But it didn't help."

"Thanks a lot!"

"No, I mean, of course you helped. It just keeps bothering me."

"You want to come over? I'm making cupcakes."

"Sweet."

We walk out together. Sterling's telling me about something that happened in gym, and I'm looking around for Derek. I feel really guilty about this, but I'd rather be with Derek than Sterling right now. Isn't that horrible?

He's waiting for me at our spot. When he sees us walking across the lawn, he smiles and waves. I wave back. Sterling is still talking and doesn't notice him.

But then she does.

She's like, "Oh. Is he waiting for you?"

"Yeah, sort of."

"Either he is or he isn't," Sterling snaps.

"He is. I'm sorry. I totally forgot we're supposed to hang out today."

"You forgot?"

Derek was walking toward us, but now he stops when he sees Sterling. It's like he can sense her anger from over there.

"Do you even *want* to come over?" Sterling accuses.

"Yes! It's just . . . I don't think I can."

"Because you'd rather be with Derek."

"No!" I don't even know what to say to her. I've never seen Sterling like this. She knows how long I've wanted a boyfriend and now I have one. So why is she acting like I'm doing something to offend her?

Sterling's all, "You're doing what we said we'd never do when we got boyfriends and I'm not feeling it."

"What am I doing?"

"You're dumping me for him. And we—"

"That is *not* true!"

"—promised we would never do that to each other."

I don't know what to say to make her stop being offended. Anyway, it's not like she can talk. She's online with random guys almost all the time now.

Derek is still waiting.

No one moves.

And then Sterling says, "Whatever. It's no big deal."

"Really?"

"Totally. I don't know what my problem is."

"Can I come over tomorrow?"

"You'd better!" She passes by Derek and says hey. I'm relieved that Sterling's not mad at me, but that was close. I've got that shaky adrenaline rush you get when a friend is all severe with you.

Derek comes over and goes, "Are you okay?"

"No." I hug him. "Hug me harder."

He squeezes me tight.

"Harder," I tell him.

"I don't want to hurt you."

I pull away a little to look at him. "Promise you'll never hurt me," I say.

Derek laughs. "Of course I'll never hurt you."

"It's not funny."

He quits laughing. "Sorry."

"I'm kind of sensitive."

"Yeah, I know. You still want to come over?"

I nod. This is just what I need. Some quality time with my amazing boyfriend. My amazing boyfriend who is going to make me feel better, make me forget how much life can suck when you least expect it.

34

Mom's like, "We need to talk."

I'm on my bed reading *Twisted*. More specifically, I'm reading a paragraph. It's the same paragraph I've read seven times already. Every time I start over, I tell myself that I have to focus because if I don't I'm going to be spending all of my time trying to read the same stupid paragraph.

"Maybe later?" I go. "I'm trying to read this."

"I'd rather talk now," Mom says.

"But this is a really good part."

"Marisa."

I look up from the book.

Mom says, "Your father's downstairs. We need to talk to you and Sandra."

"About what?"

"You'll see. It's important."

The last person I want to be is the difficult kid. I'd much rather be the balanced kid. And I don't want to give Mom a hard time forever. I just can't help still being mad at her.

Dad's sitting on the couch. Only he's not all sprawled out with his feet hanging over the edge, the way he used to be. He looks uncomfortable, like he's sitting on a couch that's not his. So he has the polite couch posture you have when you're over at a stranger's house.

He looks so out of place. I wish things would just go back to the way they were before, with all of us happy and Dad lounging on the couch, hogging the remote.

"Hey, kid," Dad says. Sandra's sitting next to him, quiet for once.

My parents exchange a look. Mom nods at Dad.

He says, "There's something we need to tell you. I thought it would be better if we were all here for this."

They look serious. This is not a good thing.

Mom goes, "We've thought a lot about this, and we think it's best—"

"I want you girls to know," Dad interrupts, "that I never wanted this to happen. But it's the only way we can move forward."

"We're getting a divorce," Mom blurts out.

They're getting a divorce. Not just a separation. They can't stand to be with each other so much that they have to make this thing permanent. Lock it down and let the whole world know.

They're just staring at me. I'm not sure what they expect me to do. Yell? Cry, like Sandra's doing? Have a screaming, hysterical fit? Whatev. They're not getting a reaction. They're not entitled to one.

I can't even look at my mom. Or my dad. She was the one who started this, but he let it happen.

35

We are sad.

We are sad and pathetic.

And we're not recovering any time soon.

Even our lunches are sad. Nash has limp spaghetti with cheap sauce. I have a soggy sandwich with rubbery cold cuts. Not that we're eating anything. We're too sad and pathetic to have an appetite. I bet if Sterling were in this lunch with us, she wouldn't even be able to tempt me with one of her famous brownies. I was so relieved when Nash's schedule changed and he showed up in my lunch this semester. Now we can be miserable together.

"At least you didn't get dumped," Nash says.

"It doesn't matter," I argue. "This still sucks."

"It sucks worse for me."

We do this sometimes. Argue about who's more depressed. All things considered, Nash wins. He's been trying to get over Rachel, but now he gets to watch her at lunch. Being all happy and laughing with her friends.

Nash looks absolutely crushed. He looks exactly how I feel.

"So what should I do about Derek?" I ask. I've already told him everything that's been going on with Sierra. "Do you think I should talk to him more and try and get him to tell me what's really going on? Or should I just believe him that nothing is?"

"I think any time something's bothering you, you should talk about it."

"But I did talk about it. He said nothing's going on."

"So maybe nothing's going on."

"But I *know* something is." I pick up my water. I put it back down. "You know how sometimes you can just tell? You have a gut feeling?"

"Then why do you have to ask?"

He has a point. If it's really true and I'm not just obsessing over nothing, then it's still true whether Derek admits it or not.

"If I were lucky enough to be Derek," Nash says, "I would never do this to you."

What did he just say?

Nash goes, "I would never even look at another girl. I would never do anything to hurt you."

Where did all *that* come from? Nash must really feel bad for me. That was so sweet. And intense. He's really . . . wow.

I'm trying to figure out what to say. Nash takes out his iPod. He selects a song, staring at the screen, not looking at me. He has one earbud in, the other one dangling down his shirt.

"What are you listening to?" I ask.

"Here." He gives me the other earbud and I put it in. I don't know what song this is, but it's extreme. I immediately love it. The iPod screen says it's called "Treasure."

I take my earbud out. "It's sad," I say.

"I know. The Cure is like that. But it always improves my mood. Misery loves company and all."

I never knew boys had songs that made them feel better. I always thought that was exclusively a girl thing.

"We should probably eat something," Nash decides.

"I know. I feel dizzy."

"I feel sick."

We stare at our food. We're not hungry. We push our trays away.

"Did you hear it last night?" Linda asks some random junior at the other end of the table.

"Dude," he says. "I always hear it."

They're obviously talking about Dirk.

Linda's like, "Can you believe it about Mrs. Hunter?"

"What a load."

"No, it's true. I mean, he never said she was the teacher who did it, but he was definitely talking about her."

"There's no way she'd do that."

"So now you're sticking up for a teacher?"

"It was probably Tabitha's fault. That chick is psycho."

They keep talking. We keep sulking.

Nash glares at Rachel for the bajillionth time.

I go, "Here, switch seats with me."

"Why?"

"Just do it." I yank Nash out of his seat and we switch so his back is to Rachel. I can't stand watching him watch her. It's heartbreaking.

I pick up my cookie. I break off a tiny piece of the edge for me and hold the cookie out to Nash. "Want?"

"Dude, no. If I eat anything, I'll vomit."

"But you already feel sick."

"That's the problem."

I rest my head on the table and look out the window. As if I don't have enough to deal with, it won't stop raining. It's rained for three days already. Three days of wet socks and bad moods and the locker room smelling like grungy mold. The rain fluctuates between drizzle and torrential. It messes with your mind. It makes you think things will always be like this, never getting better, always letting you down right when you thought the worst was over.

36

A note lands on my desk in psychology elective. I turn around to see who threw it. Julia is giving me a look.

I hold the note under my desk so Ms. Knight doesn't snatch it away. She's infamous for that kind of thing. I unfold the paper slowly, so she can't hear it crinkle. Then I peek under my desk and read it.

> Derek sat with Sierra at lunch. Just thought you should know.

There's no way. If they've been talking since the last time I saw them, why hasn't Derek told me? And how is he all of a sudden having *lunch* with her?

I glance back at Julia. She does this shruggy thing with her shoulders like, *Sorry to have to tell you.*

Why *did* she have to tell me? Unless she thought it was important. Like if she thought something was still going on between
them.

I go up to Julia after class. I'm all, "Why did you tell me this?"

"I thought you'd want to know."

"Did it look like . . ." This is so embarrassing. I don't even know
her that well and I have to ask her this. ". . . they were . . . like, that
something was going on?"

Julia doesn't say anything for a minute. She's a nice person and
I know she didn't tell me this to hurt me. So she doesn't want to
say anything I don't want to hear.

"Not really," she says. "I wasn't sitting close enough to tell,
though."

"Oh."

"I just didn't know if you knew, so . . ."

"Yeah. Thanks."

"Sorry."

I'm furious. The need to talk to Derek is burning me up. It will
be totally impossible to think about anything else until I can talk
to him and find out the truth. But I have to wait because there's
one more period left. I'm sure it was nothing.

Except if I'm so sure, why can't I stop thinking about it?

The last bell rings ten years later. I bolt out of class and get to
Derek's locker way before he does.

"Hey, sexy," Derek goes when he finally shows up. Then he hugs
me like nothing's wrong. As if I'm the only girl he's interested in.
As if he didn't just sit with Sierra at lunch.

He doesn't know I know. I want to see if he admits it on his own.

"What's up?" he says.

"Nothing much here. How about you?"

"You know how it goes. Same old same."

"So, like . . . nothing unusual happened today?"

"Where, here? Good one!" He holds my hand and starts walking, but I don't move. He looks back at me. The look doesn't look scared. It looks like not only does he not know I know, but he has no intention of telling me about his lunch date. "Ready to go?"

"Not really."

"What's wrong?"

"Did you . . . have lunch with Sierra?"

"Is that what's bothering you?" Derek laughs. "I wouldn't call it *having lunch*. She just came over to my table."

"For how long?"

"I don't know. Five minutes?"

"What did she want?"

"We were just talking, Marisa. It was nothing."

"Well, if it's so nothing, then why didn't you tell me about it?"

"Because it's nothing!" Derek drops my hand. "There's nothing to tell!"

You know that feeling you get when you know you're not hearing the whole story? Yeah. But I'll do anything to avoid a fight. So I go, "Sorry." I grab his hand. "I'm just being weird."

Derek smiles and presses his forehead against my shoulder. "Can we please forget this?"

"Forget what?" I go. Because he's right. I have a boyfriend who loves me. What else do I need? "I'm still coming over, right?"

"You know it. And we have the whole place to ourselves for"— Derek holds up our attached hands and twists his wrist so he can read his watch—"two hours and thirteen minutes. If we hurry up."

We speed walk down the hall and karoom around the corner. And there's Sierra, putting up a poster.

Of course Sierra's putting up a poster. Of course, out of all the possible people who could possibly be in the hall right now, there's Sierra. And her poster.

She's all, "Hey, you guys."

"Hey," we say back.

And that's it. No inside jokes. No secret look.

So I'm feeling a lot better. Until we get to the end of the hall. That's when Sierra yells, "Derek!"

He turns around. "Yeah?"

"Can you come here a minute?"

Derek looks at me. "If it bothers you, I won't go."

"No. Go."

He runs back down the hall. I watch them talking. Then, Derek takes the poster from Sierra and climbs up the ladder to hang it on the wall. She steps back to tell him if it's straight. This takes much longer than it should. It looks straight to me, but I'm all the way over here. I can't even hear what they're saying.

Derek gets off the ladder. Sierra says something to him. I watch him smile. I watch her touch his arm as he starts walking back to me, letting her hand brush along his arm as he turns away.

I stay quiet as we walk outside. When we get to where Derek's ride is supposed to pick us up, he's like, "Damn."

"What?"

"I can't go home yet. I forgot . . . I have to get some stuff from the library."

"That's okay. I'll go back in with you."

"But then Evan won't know where I am."

"So I'll wait here and tell him you're coming."

Evan pulls up in a ridiculous SUV. He only has his permit, so I don't think he's allowed to drive without an adult in the car. But Evan gives Derek rides home when he doesn't feel like walking.

"I don't want him to have to wait." Derek goes up to the driver's side and tells Evan that he needs to stay late. Then he calls over to me, "Do you want a ride, or—?"

"That's okay." I really don't need some random boy illegally driving me home.

"Later, dude," Derek says. Evan drives off.

And then it's just the two of us. Deciding which way to go.

Derek says, "So . . . do you still want to come in with me?"

Part of me wants to go with him. Because I have this annoying feeling that he's going back in to see Sierra. I seriously doubt he has to get anything from the library.

But my parents have always taught me the importance of trust. And if I want this thing with Derek to work, I have to trust him.

"No," I decide. "I'm walking home."

How can it feel so perfect with someone one second, but then the next second everything's suddenly all wrong?

37

Just when I thought Nash was coming out of his haze of despair, the worst thing imaginable happened to him. Rachel officially started going out with someone else. And the someone else is Edwin.

"Wait, Edwin the massive football player?" I ask when Nash breaks the news.

"The one and only," Nash mumbles.

"That's just plain flat-out wrong."

"Tell me something I don't know."

I grab a card before it flies away in the breeze. Nash taught me how to play Set, which is a logic card game that rocks. We've been hanging out a lot since Rachel broke up with Nash, playing games or just talking or doing lab reports. It's officially spring today, which usually means winter didn't get the memo about how it's supposed be getting warmer, but it's freakishly warm out and really sunny. So we decided to play Set out on the dock.

"How did you find out?" I ask.

"Darius told me when I ran into him at Shake Shack."

"Darius? Why would he care?"

"We used to be friends before he went all ghetto on our asses, remember?"

I totally forgot about that. Nash is a Mathlete and Darius was on the team until he dropped out. I heard that he tried to get back on when he snapped out of his rebel phase, but the coach wouldn't let him join again. Nash and Darius used to be good friends. I know how quickly that can change.

"It's so stupid," Nash complains. "What do they have in common, anyway? Rachel is way too smart for that Neanderthal to even comprehend what she's talking about."

"There's no way it'll last."

"How can she even like him? I thought she had more class than that."

"It's so sad."

"Are you making fun of me?"

"No! It really is sad. She totally didn't realize how lucky she was to have you."

Nash looks at me. It's one of those times when I wish I could take back what I just said. Because the thing where he tried to kiss me is out there. Me knowing that he liked me is out there. Once things like that are out there, you can never take them back.

"I have an idea," I announce. "Let's play Would You Rather."

"Now?"

"Why not? Or do you want to play more Set?"

Nash throws a twig into the river. We watch it swirl around. I squint at the bright sunlight twinkles on the water.

"Or would you rather be miserable and sulky forever?"

Nash sighs. "Fine. You start."

"Okay. Would you rather . . . um, let's see . . . would you rather be in love with one person your whole life or have lots of different relationships?"

"Is this supposed to make me feel better?"

"Sorry, I can think of something else. Okay—"

"No, I'll answer it. I'd rather have relationships with tons of different girls so I could dump them whenever I felt like it and I'd never have to know this kind of pain again."

"You don't mean that."

"How do you know?"

"Because I know you. You're not like that."

"Oh, yeah? How am I?"

"You're loyal. You'd never hurt anyone. And even if you did, it wouldn't make you feel better. You'd feel horrible about it."

Nash smiles. "Yeah. You know me."

"It's your turn."

"Would you rather rule the world for one day or get to do whatever you want for a month?"

"Are people actually going to listen to me while I'm ruling the world?"

"Yes. You can make any laws you want."

"Can I make world peace a law?"

"Yes."

"Deal."

The breeze pushes my hair back. The river sparkles all around us. I wish the Now could always be like this.

"You're up," Nash says.

"Okay . . . Would you rather have your entire bell collection get stolen or fail all of your classes for one marking period?"

"Dude." Nash thinks about it. "The bells would have to go."

"Yeah, right! You'd give up all your bells just to save your GPA for one marking period?"

"I'd have to."

"That sounds like a load of hoo-larkey."

"Um. *Hoo*-larkey?"

"Yeah. You know, like a combination of malarkey and hoo-ha."

"Malarkey? Throwback moment!"

"I'm vintage like that."

"I know. It's one of your best qualities." There's this spark of energy that passes between us and I feel like I'm not alone in the world.

We sit on the dock for a really long time. The color of the sky fades to orange. We watch the sky reflected on the water, shifting and changing, but still being sky.

38

Some people are suspecting that Kelvin is Dirty Dirk. Andrea is one of those people.

"I know it's him," she whispers. "Who else is like that?"

"We don't know Dirk's actually like that in real life," I whisper back.

"I'm telling you," she whispers fiercely, "it's him!"

Mr. Silverstein is working up a sweat. This tends to happen when we play faster pieces with a lot of complicated parts. He's working with the cellos now.

"I'm watching him," Andrea whispers.

"Who, Kelvin?"

"Yeah. I'm watching for clues."

"Like what?"

"Like anything that proves he's Dirk!"

Today is a full orchestra day, so the band geeks are playing with us. There's a new kid playing the triangle this semester. He's a freshman, so maybe he doesn't realize how dorky it is for a boy to be playing the triangle. Or anyone, really. The girl who played the triangle last semester has moved on to the wonders of the oboe. So far, I am not impressed with the new boy. He's so bad he makes the triangle sound out of tune. Which I didn't even think was possible.

"Measure six, violins!" Mr. Silverstein booms. We get into position with our bows poised above the strings.

All day I'm looking around for Dirk, searching for clues from stuff he's said during his show, trying to see if I can tell who he is. Maybe he's Kelvin, but I'm not convinced. My brain is still buzzing with possibilities after school. I can't wait to be alone with Derek, but when I open my locker a note falls out and it's from him. The note says that he's staying after for a yearbook meeting and he'll explain later. So I meet Sterling at her locker to see if she wants to do something.

"Let's go to the Notch," I say.

"I would, but I can't."

"Why not?"

"Oh. There's this thing I have to do." She's all flushed. And jittery. Like how you get when you're crushing on someone and you just saw them.

There must be a new boy.

I glance around to see if anyone cute just walked by, but there's no one she'd like.

"So," I say. "Are you ever going to tell me about your new boyfriend?"

Sterling blushes harder. "He's not my *boyfriend*," she goes. "Yet."

"Oooh! This one's a keeper!"

"Pretty much."

"What's his name?"

Sterling smiles into her locker. "Chris."

"That's a good name."

"Um-hm."

"And when do we get to meet this Chris?"

"Soon."

I don't know why she's being so secretive about him. And why I had to be the one to bring him up. Shouldn't she be dying to tell me about him? I mean, how long have we waited for both of us to have boyfriends?

I go, "Well, can the four of us hang out this weekend?"

"I'll ask."

"Don't sound too excited or anything."

"No, it's just that he's not . . . here."

"Where is he?"

"He's . . . we met online."

"Oh."

"Yeah. And he doesn't live here. He lives in New York."

"What grade is he in?"

"He's not."

"Ew, he dropped out? Sterling, you can't—"

"He didn't drop out. He finished high school."

"Like . . . last year?"

Sterling shakes her head. She goes, "He's twenty-one."

Okay. See, I'm trying to be cool about this? And understanding and all? But it's just too much. She's IMing with some creepy guy (who could actually be some middle-aged woman for all she knows) who doesn't even live here. And who is breaking the law. Or at least, wants to.

"But that's illegal," I say.

"There's nothing illegal about talking to someone. We haven't even met yet."

Yet. She's actually thinking about meeting this guy. She actually thinks that he could be her boyfriend.

"But you're going to meet eventually," I say. "And then what?"

"I don't know. All I know is that he's way more mature than any of the rejects I've gone out with. Look, I know I need a lot of attention. But Chris understands. He just wants to take care of me. So what if he's older—that's what I want. I need way more affection than some lame sixteen-year-old boy can give."

You know how people talk about red flags? And how if you see one, it means stay away from that boy? I'm seeing a whole troop of red flags, flapping wildly and screaming, *Danger!*

"I have to say," Sterling goes, "I was getting really afraid that no one could ever love me enough. Like maybe it was me, you know? But Chris sees me for who I really am. And he cares about me. And he's always there, whenever I need him."

She's for real. She's seriously falling for some creepy online guy. And there's nothing I can do about it. Because one thing I've learned is this: When you're falling in love, no one can stop you. No matter what.

I follow her outside. "Fine," I go. "But just so you know, I'm keeping score of how many times you blow me off."

"I'm not blowing you off."

"I'm not arguing over semantics."

"I just have to go, is all."

"So go." I'm seriously ticked off by the whole thing. Doesn't she know he could be some deranged lunatic?

Sterling doesn't go. She drops her bag on the ground and says, "Can I ask you something?"

"Since when do you ask if you can ask?"

"I know, but . . . when did you first tell Derek that you loved him?"

"On Valentine's Day, right after he told me. Remember?"

"Oh, yeah."

"Why?"

Her eyes get all far away and foggy. "No reason . . ."

And then I get it. Sterling and Chris must have been talking for a while by now.

The whole thing is so stupid. She's avoiding plans with real people to go home and IM with some sketchy concept of a guy. She's directing all her energy toward a fantasy that she's treating as reality. So what if Chris IMs with her every day (usually more than once, apparently) while I sometimes don't have a real conversation with Derek until the weekend? At least I know who I'm talking to.

I have a bad feeling about all of this and where it's going, but I don't want Sterling to get mad at me. And if I keep telling her what I really think, that's exactly what's going to happen. So I hold this in, adding it to all the other stuff I know I should say but won't.

39

Sierra asked Derek to join yearbook and he said yes. Oh, and he told me over IM.

thederek: i'm joining yearbook.

f-stop: why?

thederek: it sounds interesting. and it'll look good on college
    apps.

f-stop: but what are you even going to do there?

thederek: um, normal things people on yearbook do? like put
    together the yearbook?

f-stop: i'm the one who should be on yearbook. they asked me
    to be a photographer but i said no.

thederek: why'd you say no?

f-stop: because i didn't want to be on yearbook!

thederek: okay, but i do.

f-stop: what's the real reason?

thederek: i already told you.

f-stop: please. i highly doubt you'd be joining yearbook if sierra
    weren't on it.

thederek: are you starting with this crap again? i told you.
    NOTHING'S GOING ON.

thederek: why don't you believe me?

f-stop: maybe because i have a hard time believing you'd want
    to be friends with someone you don't even like anymore.

thederek: when did i say that?

f-stop: derek. you've told me a million times how she's the one
    who comes up to you and you don't even want to talk to her.
    like that time in lunch.

thederek: that was ONE time. you really need to move on.

He's the one who needs to move on. Which is highly unlikely
now that they're both on yearbook. That means lots of days after
school together. Working in that small office, all up close and personal. I keep getting these images in my head of them scrunched
up together in front of a computer screen, deciding which pictures
to choose. Remembering their history. Getting closer.

There's only one person who can pull me out of this quick-
sand. I know I need to be with him because I can't be alone right
now. So I text him that we need an emergency movie evening,
and he texts back that I'm a genius and I should meet him at his
house. When I get there, his dad answers the door.

"Hi, Marisa." He moves to the side so I can come in. "Nash
should be back soon."

"Thanks."

"Can I get you something to drink?"

"No, I'm good."

His dad nods thoughtfully, pondering this profound statement.

"Well," Mr. Parker eventually says. He checks his watch. "He should be back any minute. You can wait . . . do you want to wait for him down here? Or up in his room, maybe?"

"Sure, Mr. Parker, I'll go up." It's so weird with Nash's dad. It's like he never knows what to do with me. I always get the feeling that I make him uncomfortable. Maybe when Nash's mom left so suddenly, he fell into this post-traumatic hole where he can't deal with girls anymore.

When I push open the door to Nash's room, some of his bells hanging from the ceiling chime. His bells are everywhere. I try to remember how many bells he had the first time I saw his room in fourth grade. I can't. But he's definitely added to his collection since then.

The only part of his bed that's semi-made is the bottom right corner. I sit on that and look around. His room is way bigger than mine, which I always get jealous about. But he's so messy! If I had a huge room like this, there's no way I would leave everything out the way he does. You can't even see that there's a desk under all the stuff piled on it.

Mr. Parker knocks on the open door and says, "How's school going?"

"Good."

"Are you thinking about college choices?"

"Not yet."

"It's never too early. It's a different world now—everything's so competitive."

"I've heard."

"Nash likes CalTech. They have an excellent robotics program."

I didn't know Nash was already thinking about college. And I didn't know he wanted to major in robotics. Is that even a real major? I guess it would technically be engineering or something like that. But I can't believe Nash never told me he's already planning this stuff.

Mr. Parker flips through some DVDs sitting by the TV. "He stays up too late watching these. My fault for getting him a TV."

"Yeah, I'm the same way."

He smiles. "I guess all kids are. Same with putting off homework till the last minute and staying out late, huh?"

"I thought Nash couldn't stay out late."

"Well, on weekends."

"Oh. I thought he had a ten thirty curfew every night."

"What?" Nash's dad obviously has no idea what I'm talking about.

"Doesn't he . . . have a ten thirty curfew?"

"No. I trust him. As long as he keeps his grades up, I'm happy." The phone rings. "Excuse me," he says. He taps on the door frame on his way out.

Why would Nash lie to me like that? Why would he want to come home early when he could be out having fun?

Weird.

And why is his desk so freaking messy? I'm sure his dad's desk looks even worse. I suddenly feel bad for Nash, like life has cheated him somehow.

I take all of the books scattered on his desk and pile them neatly on the side. I'm about to organize all these folders that are lying around when I notice a familiar paper stuck under a *South Park* desk calendar (that hasn't been flipped since school started) and some headphones. The reason this paper is familiar is because it's mine.

In seventh grade, I traced my hand with a silver pen on black stationery and wrote all my favorite song lyrics inside the tracing. Then I slid the paper into the clear cover of my binder. One day, the paper was gone. I thought it just slipped out because the cover was really loose by then. But I didn't lose that paper after all. It's right here on Nash's desk.

I had no idea he liked me for so long.

Then I panic that Nash is about to come in and see that I found it, so I hide the paper back where it was.

"Hey, sorry," Nash says. He's out of breath. "I ran like halfway home." He crashes on his bed, panting.

"What happened to you?"

"Crazy story. Have you been here long?"

"No. Like fifteen minutes."

"Sorry about that."

"You have a lot of bells."

"Have we just met?"

"No, I mean you've gotten a lot more since the first time I came over. Remember that? In fourth grade?"

"Yeah."

"Or maybe I haven't met you yet."

"How metaphysical of you. I'm Nash."

"Marisa."

We shake.

"You ready for emergency movie evening?" he says.

"Could not possibly *be* more ready."

While Nash selects a movie from his massive collection, I look around his room in a new way, instead of just dismissing it as a messy boy room. I love how it always feels like home to me. And how you can see everything that's happened since we played together when we were little, like it's all preserved in a time capsule. There's one of those plastic bracelets we used to have to wear at the beach. Spin art from the River Ramble. That family tree project we had to do last year. It's like a time line of our parallel lives, how we experienced the same things. This bittersweet nostalgia of all the times we'll never live again. It's intense.

Intense in a good way. Because I have all of these memories and I'll never let them go. They'll become part of who I am, who I turn out to be when I'm older. And they're the same memories that are part of Nash, too.

40

I'm psyched that it's spring break, which is earlier than usual this year. Every year when it's finally spring, we have the River Ramble. It's this kind of carnival that's set up on the first weekend of April on the boardwalk along the river. There are rides and food and games, and even if you're too old for it, you have to go. It's tradition. There's even a section of tables set up for bingo.

Before Derek joined yearbook, we would hang out after school almost every day at his house or mine, watching TV and making out. Now I'm lucky if I get to see him twice a week. Even though it's break so we can see each other more, I don't know if he's going to be here today. He hates these dorky town events, as he calls them. So I told Nash I'd meet him by the Ferris wheel.

I watch families wandering around. It's so weird being at these things now, with everyone knowing that my parents are getting divorced. I watch a little boy with his parents. He looks so happy, just being here with them. I remember coming here with my parents and Sandra when we were little. I must have looked just as happy as that little boy. Now everything's ruined and there's no way to fix it.

Nash shows up and I instantly feel way better just seeing him. It's like magic.

He looks up at the Ferris wheel. "Should we ride it?"

"I don't think so." Ferris wheels can be fun, but this portable one looks so chintzy.

We head toward the game where you have to pop balloons with a dart. Nash likes that one. I remember seeing him here last year and how he totally hogged that booth. It's weird how I can remember the most random things, but then I'll forget other things that are way more important.

Nash doesn't stop at the balloons.

I go, "I thought you liked the balloons."

"I do. But I'd rather play bingo."

"Yeah, right."

"No, I'm serious."

I look at him. He looks serious.

"Oh, well . . . I guess that could be fun. We could—"

But then Nash cracks up. "I can't keep a straight face! It's too easy!"

I swat his arm. "Ha-ha."

We watch the bingo game anyway. There are some hard-core ladies playing. One old lady has like ten blotters in all different colors set up in a semicircle around her cards. A lot of people have lucky charms and toys in their areas.

Nash goes, "Remember that time you stood up yelling that you had bingo, but then you didn't really have it?"

"Good one. Except I never played bingo."

"Yes, you did."

"No, I *didn't*."

"How can you not remember?"

"Um, maybe because I only remember things that actually happened?"

"You yelled out that you had bingo and you were all jumping up and down and waving your card around. And then the checker came over and there was one space she didn't call that you'd marked."

"Wait, was that like in seventh grade?"

"Aha! It's all coming back to you."

"Oh my god." He's right. I did play one game as a joke or a dare or something. I remember the old ladies looking at me like I was ruining their party. I felt bad after. "I can't believe you remember that!"

"Oh, I remember. Big-time."

"But I just did it on a dare. Or something."

"Right, right."

"I'm serious!" I swat him again.

"Dude, what is it with you and smacking me?"

"I was just wondering the same thing," Derek says. Who is suddenly behind us.

I'm like, "What are you—when did you get here?"

"A while ago."

Nash is like, "Yeah . . . I have some balloons to pop with my professional dart skills, so . . ."

"I'll find you later," I go.

Derek just glares at him. Nash could not leave fast enough.

I'm like, "What?"

"Are you always like that with him?"

"Like what?"

"All flirty?"

"I wasn't flirting. God! Nash was just bugging me because he said that I—"

"Whatever. I know what I saw."

"Like you can talk."

"What's that supposed to mean?"

"You're not even really here when you're here."

"The only reason I'm here is because you wanted me to come."

Lately when I'm with Derek, it feels like he's somewhere else or he wants to be somewhere else and he has to settle for being with me instead. As if I'm a consolation prize. And it doesn't matter how many times he says he wants to be with me or that he doesn't want to be with Sierra, it just doesn't feel like the truth.

"I know," I say, "it just feels like . . . like you're thinking about other things a lot of the time."

"So are you."

"Not the way you are."

"Look. I'm not a mind reader. If there's something you want me to know, you have to tell me."

"I need you to be here for me and it doesn't feel like you are."

"Then where am I?"

"Yearbook!"

"Is that what this is about? Again?"

"You're always staying after. I never see you during the week anymore."

"If you want to hang out more, why didn't you just say so?"

"I didn't want to have to tell you. I wanted you to want to. Without me forcing you to."

"Why would you think I'd have to be forced to spend time with my girlfriend?"

I want to say, *Which one?* But I don't. I know I'm being a bitch. But I can't help it. It's like some force I can't control has taken over my personality and turned me into this obsessive, paranoid freak. Who can't be trusted to play nice in social environments.

Here's what I don't want to admit: I'm scared. Because I recognize this feeling. The last time I felt like this, it was right before my major meltdown. And there was no way to stop the anxiety and depression from taking over my life, turning me into someone I never wanted to be. The same person I'm struggling never to become again.

Derek goes, "How do you think it makes me feel to see you with Nash?"

"We're just friends."

"Yeah, but so are me and Sierra."

"But you guys used to go out. I never went out with Nash."

"But you go to him with your problems, right?"

He's right. It's partly because I don't want to bother Derek. No one wants to be with someone who always has problems.

Is Derek actually jealous of Nash? Is that even possible?

"I don't want to fight with you," Derek says.

"I know. I don't either."

"Then why are you doing this?"

I wish I knew. Am I making a big deal over a problem that doesn't even exist?

"Sorry," I say. "I just miss you."

"We're still on for tomorrow, right?"

"Yeah."

I want to believe that everything will be okay. But maybe it never is. Maybe there is no one perfect person and anyone you end up with will eventually make you think there's someone better out there.

41

Over the next few days, I focus on being creative and calming my Derek anxiety. I develop two rolls of film. I write a new wall section. I practice violin. Bonus: Sandra doesn't hassle me while I'm practicing in the bathroom.

No major catastrophes have occurred. I've seen my dad a few times. This annoying girl from work quit. Most of my teachers assigned homework over break, but a lot of it is already done. Nash and I have hung out every day. And Derek said he wants to get together more.

He's over now, holding a pen in front of my face. It has sparkles and pink feathers on it.

"Ooh!"

"I knew you'd like it."

"Are you kidding? I love it!"

"Cool."

"Where'd you get it?"

"Alphabets. It was the last one."

"Thanks." Only Derek would do something so sweet for me. I don't know if all boyfriends are like this, but if they're not, they definitely should be.

"Hey," he says. "What are you doing Saturday?"

"Finishing that stupid stock market project."

"I haven't even started that thing," Derek confesses. "I was planning to do it Sunday night."

"Seriously?"

"Yeah. Why not?"

"Well . . . it's a lot of work. I've already spent two days on it."

"Guess I'm screwed."

"Sorry."

"No worries. You can make it up to me."

"How?"

"By hanging out with me Saturday night."

Why is he asking me this? He knows Sterling and I have our standing date every Saturday night. "I can't."

"Why not?"

I give him a look like, *You already know why not.* "It's Saturday? I'm already doing something with Sterling."

"But this is really important. Evan's band is playing and I said we'd go."

"What about Sterling?"

"What *about* her?" Derek has tone. "It's not like you have to spend every single Saturday night with her, is it?"

"Well, yeah. I kind of do."

"Why?"

"Because we promised!"

"But wasn't that some deal like where you'd go out on Saturdays until you had boyfriends?"

"Exactly! Does Sterling have a boyfriend?" I don't count Chris as an actual person.

"No, but you do."

"So how fair would it be for me to ditch her like that?"

"I'm sure she'd understand."

"She'd understand I'm a bad friend is what she'd understand."

"Dude," Derek says. "If you don't want to go, just tell me."

"No, I do."

"So we're going."

How can I possibly tell Sterling? If the tables were turned and she did this to me? I'd definitely be mad. What makes me think she won't feel the same way?

But what if she never has a boyfriend? Do I have to keep going out with her every single Saturday night until we graduate?

Derek's right. I'm sure she'll understand just this once. But when I call her, I'm still nervous.

Sterling says, "What movie are we seeing Saturday?"

"We need to talk about that."

"Oh, no. I am *not* seeing that part three whatever rah-rah."

"That's not it. It's . . . I can't go."

"Huh?"

"I'm going out with Derek."

"On Saturday?"

"Yeah."

"*Our* Saturday?"

"I know, but—"

"I knew this would happen," Sterling says.

"What?"

"I knew you wouldn't be able to stick with me. The second you got a boyfriend, everything started changing."

"That's not true!"

"Yes, it is. You just can't see it because you're the one who's in it."

Okay, I felt bad before? But now she's getting me mad. "I didn't know I wasn't allowed to make other plans," I say.

"And I didn't know you wanted to."

"I don't. It's—I can't go out with you every single Saturday, is all."

"Gee, I'm sorry it's been such a sacrifice for you. I was under the impression that you liked spending time with me."

"I do! You know that."

"Umm. I thought I did. But now I think Chris was right about you."

Oh, no he didn't. Some creepy online guy is talking trash about me when he doesn't even *know* me?

I'm like, "Don't take this the wrong way, because I think it's great that you're so excited about talking to this guy Chris and everything, it's just . . . you don't even know him. You don't know what he's really like."

"I *do* know him. I know he's sweet and caring and funny and we have a lot in common. So I really don't appreciate you being all weirded out by it."

"I'm sorry. I'm just worried about you."

"Or maybe you're just jealous."

"*Jealous?* Of what?"

"Um, I don't know, maybe because I have a boyfriend who actually notices me?"

"Boyfriend? You don't even know him!"

"Will you quit saying that?" Sterling yells. "I know Chris a lot better than you know Derek!"

"Sterling—"

"I keep giving you chances. I keep thinking things will get better, but they just keep getting worse."

"No, they don't!"

"I gotta go," she says.

And then she hangs up on me.

42

The next day, I expect Sterling to call and say she's sorry. But that doesn't happen. She doesn't call or IM or text or anything. When we go back to school, Sterling's all clinging to these girls from French Club. They're the same girls we used to make fun of and say how stuck-up they were. I guess Sterling forgot about that. Or maybe she doesn't care. When I pass her in the hall, she looks away. She's so angry. Which I feel horrible about, but what did I do? Get a boyfriend? As if she doesn't want Chris to be hers.

Oh. And another thing? Is that Sterling dyed her hair back to brown.

I try to forget about it and focus on my other friends, the way Sterling's doing. Like today, Derek and I are hanging out after school with Evan and Julia. Everyone was wondering when they'd finally start going out. We've only hung out with them once before, which was kind of lame because I don't have anything in common with either of them. There's never anything to talk about. Sometimes it's a struggle to think of stuff to say around Julia.

She's good at bowling, though. So after school the four of us go to Cosmic Bowling, where they turn off the lights and the lanes light up. They have glow-in-the-dark bowling balls and black lights, so all the bowling shoes have white stripes on them. They even have strobe lights and a fog machine.

Maybe we just needed an activity other than doing nothing, because I'm having a blast. It's boys against girls and we're actually winning.

"Do-over!" Evan yells at me.

"No way!" I yell back. "That was totally legal."

"Your shoe crossed the line."

"It did not!"

"Yuh-huh!"

I stick my tongue out at him.

"Really mature," Evan taunts.

"I think it was in," Derek says.

"My hero," I coo.

And then we're kind of just standing there, all googly eyes and cheesy smiles.

Julia goes, "Y'all want us to leave, or . . . ?"

"No, we're done," Derek says, still googly.

The song changes and the lights flicker with the beat.

"That's my *song*, yo!" Evan yells. He busts out this ridiculous dance move that cracks us up.

I brought my camera. Every time I go bowling I'm like, *I have to bring my camera next time,* and then I always forget. But this time, I remembered.

When Derek goes up to roll, I point the lens at him.

"Are you getting a good angle?" Derek says. He bends over. "How about this?"

"Nice," Julia says.

Evan glares at her.

"What?" she says. "I can't look?"

"No, you can't," Evan says. "Anyway, why would you want to when you have me?"

"Yes!" Derek goes. "Strike!"

I shoot a roll of film. I can't wait to see how the photos come out, so I develop them as soon as I get home. They're righteous. There's one I took of Derek that's kind of blurry, the lights a smudge of purple and blue behind him. I love it. So when it's done, I take it up to my room and slip it into my new binder cover. Time ticks away as I sit on my bed, decorating my binder around the picture of him.

Sandra walks into my room through our bathroom.

"You could knock," I say.

"You could be less of a dork," she says.

"Talking to yourself again?"

"You wish." Sandra sits on my bed and looks at my binder. "Who's that?"

"Duh! Derek?" I turn the binder around so she can see it. "See?"

"Oh. It's kind of blurry."

"That's the point."

"Why would you want a blurry picture on your binder?"

"It's an artistic choice. Did you want something?"

Sandra gets fidgety in that way she does when she's about to ask me something big. So far, she's asked me how to use a tampon and some sex stuff. It's not like we don't talk to Mom, but it's way less embarrassing to talk to each other.

"Say a boy always teases you," Sandra goes. "Does that mean he likes you or hates you?"

"Who's teasing you?"

"It's a hypothetical question."

"I see."

"So . . . what does it mean?"

"Well, it depends on how he's teasing you. Hypothetically."

"Let's assume he sits behind you in a class. Like physical science. And he's always poking you. And when you turn around, he pretends he didn't poke you. Is he just being annoying, or would that mean he likes me—the person?"

Was my life ever that simple? Where my biggest problem was whether some immature boy liked me?

"I would say he likes you. I mean, the person. The hypothetical person." I'm trying really hard not to laugh. "Because if he didn't, then why would he be paying so much attention to this person?"

"I know, right? That's what I thought."

"Not that I'm an expert or anything."

"You know about these things. You have a boyfriend."

Derek looks so cute in this photo. The blur somehow makes him look even cuter.

Sandra says, "Okay, so . . . say, hypothetically, this person might possibly like the boy who's teasing her. What should she do?"

"Um . . . how about nothing because she's not old enough to date yet?"

"I am, too!"

"Says who?"

"Dad."

"You asked Dad if you're allowed to go out on dates?"

"No, but I will."

"When? I want to be there for that one."

"When I know for sure that he likes me."

"Does he have a name, or are we going to keep pretending he's not real?"

"That's all the information you will be receiving at this time," Sandra informs me in a crisp tone. Then she whisks back into her room with an official air.

I pick up my binder and kiss blurry Derek. We had so much fun today. It felt exactly like when we first started going out, when everything was perfect and we had zero problems. And just because he's on yearbook with Sierra doesn't mean anything serious is going on with them. She might like him, but love goes both ways.

My IM signal pings.

dorkbot10013: Busy?

f-stop: not really

dorkbot10013: Did you do your English paper?

f-stop: ugh! no. you?

dorkbot10013: Mine's been done for two days.

f-stop: could you BE any more annoying?

dorkbot10013: It's a possibility. What did you have in mind?

f-stop: ha ha

dorkbot10013: What are you doing Saturday night?

f-stop: i'm booked.

dorkbot10013: With what?

f-stop: i have plans with derek.

dorkbot10013: What happened to your Saturday nights with
    Sterling?

f-stop: we're not speaking.

dorkbot10013: Why not?

f-stop: it's complicated. mostly, it's because she hates me now.

dorkbot10013: That's harsh.

f-stop: ☹

dorkbot10013: What did you do?

f-stop: nothing! why do you automatically assume it's my fault?

dorkbot10013: Well, why does she suddenly hate you?

f-stop: i told you. it's complicated.

dorkbot10013: But you're busy Saturday.

f-stop: yeah.

dorkbot10013: I guess I can't ask you, then.

f-stop: ask me what?

dorkbot10013: To come with me to the Dorkbot finals.

f-stop: *gasp* shut up!

dorkbot10013: It's Saturday at 8.

f-stop: i'm so there.

dorkbot10013: What about Derek?

f-stop: he'll understand.

dorkbot10013: Are you sure?

f-stop: just tell me where to meet you.

dorkbot10013: I'll pick you up.

f-stop: oooh! like a datebot!

dorkbot10013: (no response)

f-stop: that was a joke.

dorkbot10013: Oh! Now I get it.

f-stop: i can hear your sarcasm through the screen.

dorkbot10013: Good, then it's working.

f-stop: ☺

dorkbot10013: Hey, good luck with that paper.

f-stop: i hate you.

dorkbot10013: The feeling is mutual.

43

When I told Nash that Derek would understand about going to the Dorkbot finals on Saturday, I was sort of lying. Because I knew he'd be mad. He didn't say much when I told him I was going—just that I'd be missing a good time—but it was so worth it. The projects at Dorkbot were amazing. There was this really cute one called Warm Fuzzy. It was a heart pillow that lit up in different colors according to your mood when you squeezed it. For his project, Nash made this motion detector that can power small appliances instead of using batteries or electricity. It blows my mind that he actually made something so complex. He totally should have won instead of coming in third place.

Ms. Maynard put us in random pairs in global today because she said we were goofing off too much in our groups. I got put with Tabitha. Everyone's complaining because we have to do graphs for this activity and we're only supposed to do graphs in science and math. So then Ms. Maynard tries to explain about concepts that are universal to all subjects and blah di blah blah, but no one cares.

Tabitha says, "How did you set up your x-axis?"

"I put time there."

"No, I know, but how did you divide your . . . make your divisions?"

"The increments?"

"Yeah, those."

"I went by fives, with two little lines in between."

Tabitha leans over my paper. "Oh," she says. "That's what I was going to do."

"I think it's the best way, because if you count—"

"Yeah, ten would be too much."

"They wouldn't fit."

"Um-hm." I can never tell how much Tabitha understands. Like, she'll say she gets something, but then she always has this blank look. As if she's waiting for you to explain more. But she never comes out and says she's stuck.

We do our graphs.

"So, yeah," Tabitha says. "You should have come to Evan's show. It was hot."

"I couldn't go."

"So I heard."

"From who?"

"Why? Is it classified information?"

I think that's Tabitha's idea of a joke. I'm never sure with her. I can't quite grasp her sense of humor.

"Not really," I say.

"No, Derek told me."

"Oh."

When I got home from the Dorkbot finals, I called Derek and got his voice mail. I left a message. He never called back. Well, he called back Sunday afternoon when he woke up and said his phone was off all night.

"I didn't know he was still hanging out with Sierra," Tabitha says.

"What?"

"They went to the after party together."

"Are you sure?" That can't be right. Derek probably just ran into her there.

"Well, they came in together and left together so, yeah, I'm pretty sure."

There's no way that's true.

Except, what if it is?

"Sorry to be the one to tell you," Tabitha adds.

I go up to Ms. Maynard and get the bathroom pass. I know where Derek is and this can't wait until after class.

I sneak down the hall to his classroom and stand outside the door so the kids can see me but the teacher can't. I find Derek, but he's not looking my way. A few other kids notice me, which means the teacher is going to realize someone's standing here in a few seconds. I don't have a lot of time.

Rachel is looking at me. I signal for her to get Derek. She throws her pencil at him.

Derek whips his head around. Rachel points to me. When Derek sees me, I motion for him to come out. I'm about to be exposed, so I run around the corner and wait.

A few minutes later, Derek comes out. He's like, "What's going on?"

"Did you go to Evan's show with Sierra?"

"What?"

"Last Saturday. Did you go to the after party with her?"

"No. Who told you that?"

"It doesn't matter."

"It kind of does, since someone's lying about it."

"Then why did it look like you went with her?"

"I don't know. She was there, but so were a lot of other people. It was a group thing."

"Did you leave with her?"

"No." Derek rubs his face. "Whatever, some of us went out for pizza after."

"Oh, and by some of you, do you mean she was included?"

"Yeah, but a bunch of us went."

"Why didn't you tell me?"

"Because I knew you'd freak out."

"Why would you think that?"

"Because that's exactly what you're doing!"

"I'm not freaking out, I'm just asking."

"No, you're accusing me of something I didn't do."

"And what's that?"

"Going to the show with Sierra!"

"You just told me that you didn't leave with her and then you said you did. Which is it?"

"Okay, now you're being crazy." Derek moves closer to me. "Why are you being so crazy?"

"When someone tells me that my boyfriend went out with his ex, I guess that makes me upset. But it's not crazy. Anyone else would feel the same way."

"Well, I didn't go with her. She was just there. It was nothing."

It was not nothing. It was obviously something that he felt he needed to hide.

When you're with someone and he really wants to be with you in this way where it's like you're the only girl in the world for him, then it's obvious and everyone feels it. Even people watching you walking down the street feel it. You radiate this kind of happiness that's infectious, like sunshine. It's like you light up the whole world just from your own euphoric glow.

And then there's me. I'm the opposite of sunshine. I'm a thunderstorm. A growling, perpetual thunderstorm, where the threat of rain never goes away and every day is bleak.

"I'm going back to class," I say.

Even though it's kind of mean, it makes me feel better to know that other people are suffering, too. Like Dirk. Because Dirk's identity has been revealed.

Dirk is really Kelvin.

Last night Dirk ranted about how we're trashing the planet. He totally dissed our country's environmental policies and complained about how our school doesn't even recycle. Which are exactly the kinds of things that Kelvin always complains about. Another clue is that Dirk plays these underground New York bands that no one's ever heard of, and Kelvin always talks about seeing all these cool bands when he lived there. He was even saying how he knew the lead singer from this band Dirk played the night before.

Ever since the show when Dirk read a super-confidential letter that the principal wrote, some school administrators have been listening, waiting for him to slip so they can catch him. And now they're convinced he's Kelvin.

Except Kelvin doesn't agree.

"It's not me," Kelvin tells us in global. He burst in late after I came back to class and now he's just standing in front of the room. Ms. Maynard lets him talk. "But whoever he is, he rocks."

I'm not convinced. That could just be Kelvin complimenting himself.

"Can I tell you how a roomful of administrators just locked me in the principal's office and drilled me?" he says.

Of course, we all want to know what happened with that. So Kelvin tells us how he got called into the principal's office and was questioned for, like, an hour. The principal threatened to have his room searched if he didn't stop broadcasting his show. Kelvin told him that he's not allowed to search his room without a warrant, but the principal said getting one wouldn't be a problem.

"That is a *complete* violation of privacy," Kelvin says. "Even if I was Dirk, which I'm not."

I can't believe Kelvin was just treated that way. Maybe the

principal assumed that if he really was Dirk, he wouldn't tell anyone about the interrogation.

Of course, everyone is ultra-ready for Dirk to come on that night. And right at eleven, he does.

"Okay, people," Dirk starts. "Evidently, there's been some debate about my identity. Someone has been falsely accused of being me. Trust me, I wouldn't wish that on my worst enemy. But rest assured, Kelvin Rodriguez and Dirty Dirk are separate entities. And to prove it, let's give him a call."

Dirk calls Kelvin. I'm not sure if he called Kelvin earlier to tell him the plan, but Kelvin answers right away. He's all, "Yo, Dirk, what's good?"

"Chillaxin'."

"A'ight."

"So I hear Mr. Principal Man gave you some inhumane treatment today."

"And on school grounds, Dirk."

"That's just wrong."

"Extremely wrong."

"Profoundly wrong."

"Could not have *been* more wrong."

"Will you be reporting him to the school board?"

"Hmm. You know, I think I might! Do you think he's listening?"

"Oh, I *know* he's listening."

"Oooh, let's talk about him some more!"

"Now, now, Kelvin. That would be stooping to his level. Someone has to be the adult around here."

I love it. I mean, I guess there's a chance some technological enhancement could be going on and Kelvin really is Dirk, but I don't think so. And I don't think anyone will ever figure out who Dirk is. He's obviously covered his tracks really well. Which I totally respect, but at the same time I'm wondering if he's okay with never getting recognition for being who he actually is. But maybe that's not his goal. Maybe his goal is to help other people in whatever way he can, just doing this. Maybe that's enough to make him happy.

44

I magine this. You're married to the love of your life. You have two kids and a great job and everything seems too perfect to be true. And then you realize it is.

The person you were married to for almost twenty years has been having an affair. Your kids aren't in your life the way they used to be. And the house you've lived in all this time is a distant memory.

Dad's condo complex looks exactly like an enormous pair of dice. They're these two big, blocky buildings, painted white with black circles here and there. Who designs something like this? Didn't they realize they were designing a big pair of dice? The whole thing is warped. And the fact that my dad lives here now is beyond warped.

Visiting Dad has gotten less strange, but it still feels like I'm in a movie or something, playing the role of the girl whose dad moved out. Sometimes Sandra and I both come over, but today it's just me. Sitting on his new couch, I'm impressed that he obviously cleaned for my visit. But underneath the sunlight and colorful couch pillows, there's something cold and lonely. It's sad that he has to live here, away from us. All closed off in this impersonal box while everything he used to love is twenty minutes away.

"Do you want something to drink?" Dad asks from the kitchen, which is actually the other side of the living room.

"Okay. What do you have?"

"What *don't* I have?" He whips open the refrigerator door to reveal an abundance of beverages. "We have apple juice, grape juice, iced tea, Jones soda, orange soda—"

"Why do you have so many drinks?"

"I get thirsty sometimes."

"Obviously." I scan the endless rows of bottles and cans.

Dad goes, "Thanks for coming over."

"Thanks for wanting me over."

We go down to the beach and walk to the lighthouse. It's this thing we've been doing for as long as I can remember. There's a quote I heard a long time ago, something my dad told me. It's about how you're like a lighthouse, always searching far into the distance. But the thing you're looking for is usually close to you and always has been. That's why you have to look within yourself to find answers instead of searching beyond.

I cuff my jeans and take off my flip-flops so I can walk in the water. It's way too cold, so I retreat to the dry sand. Dad walks on the wet sand.

"How are things at home?" Dad asks.

"Bad."

"You shouldn't blame your mother."

That's even sadder than his apartment. Dad calling Mom "your mother." That's what one parent says when they hate the other one.

"How can you be so nice about this?" I go. "Aren't you mad?"

Dad picks up one of those smooth, black stones he likes. He still collects the black ones and I still collect the white ones.

"I was mad at first," he says. "But not anymore."

"Why not?"

"It wasn't really about forgiving her for her benefit. I needed to forgive her so I could move on. And time helps."

I know he's right, but I don't get it. How can things go away and feelings change so drastically just because some time passed by? How can time change what happened?

We walk some more. I find three white stones. I put them in my pocket, where they'll be safe.

"Your mother's trying," Dad says. "You should give her a chance."

I want to be the kind of person who can do that. Move on and forgive people and be healthy and happy. It seems like an easy thing to do in my head. But it's not so easy when you try it in real life.

45

This life thing is just too hard.

Like right now? All I can do is lie here on my bed, staring out the window. I can't make myself do the simplest things anymore. Like get out of bed, go to my desk, and start my homework. I can already tell tonight is going to be a total failure. Just like every other night this week.

I haven't been doing my homework. Sometimes I do some of it, the easier assignments and stuff, but most of it isn't getting done. And it's like there's nothing I can do about it. Somewhere under all this pain I want to do my homework, but that wanting is a tiny light far away that I can barely see. I'm slipping and there's nothing to grab on to. It's a scary, horrible feeling to be trapped in your own body when all you want to do is get out.

Every night, I sit in front of the TV for hours. It's all I do now. I've only seen Derek one day this week. The rest of the time he's stayed after for yearbook or whatever. So I stare at the TV, ignoring the homework I know I'm going to feel awful about not doing tomorrow. I can feel the depression pulling me under and it's way easier to drown than to fight it.

I'm tired. Really tired. The kind of tired you can feel in your bones. I'm sleeping eleven or twelve hours a night, sometimes more on weekends. The first thing I do when I get home from school is crash on my bed and sleep until dinner. Then I watch TV until it's time to go to sleep again.

My mom's in her own world and can't see how things are changing around her. She gave up on convincing me to forgive her, which is how she always reacts when I give her attitude for long enough. Dad can take it for as long as I can bring it, but Mom crumples under that kind of pressure. I'm sure she's happier now, not worrying about me anymore. It gives her more time to focus on Jack. And most nights she gets home really late, so she doesn't know how bad I'm feeling. Or maybe she can sense it and she's avoiding me on purpose. Maybe she thinks depression is contagious. So Mom's being more distant when I need her the most. But I'm too tired to clue her in. And I just don't have the energy to talk to Dad.

I'm fading away into my nap. Except this time, just when I'm drifting off to sleep, I snap my eyes open. This is no way to live. I have to fight this if I want to survive. There's no way I'm sinking back into the darkness.

I swing my legs over the side of my bed and sit up. My head hurts. Plus I'm dizzy. Maybe I have a brain tumor. I probably have a brain tumor and only two more days to live. What would you do if you only had two more days to live? Then again, if you're going to die anyway, what's the point? It's not going to matter what you did before if you're dead.

There's a pink fluffy thing on my wall. I don't even remember putting it there. I hate pink fluffy things. I want to burn all pink fluffy things.

My room looks like someone else lives here. Did I seriously hang up all of this junk on my walls? It's making me even dizzier, seeing all of the collages and writing and posters and photos and . . . what *is* all this?

I start with the corner of one wall that has the most collage action. I start ripping everything down.

Sandra's like, "What are you doing?"

"Go away." Oh, that's another thing. I'm in this perpetual stank mood. It's like I'm annoyed with everybody, even when they're just trying to help.

Sandra is unfazed. She goes, "Why are you ripping your stuff down?"

"Don't you ever knock?"

"Maybe when the door's not already open." She watches me yank a collage apart. "But it took you so long to do that!" she yells.

"I can hear you. You don't have to yell."

"You're crazy! Why are you doing that?"

"I'm redecorating."

"Are you repainting? Because Mom already asked you if you wanted to repaint when I—"

"When you redid your room last year, I know." Sandra's still bitter because she picked out a color that she supposedly loved and then she decided she loved a different color way more after her walls were already repainted. But Mom wouldn't let her change the color because the paint was expensive. So whenever she doesn't get her way, Sandra still brings up the travesty of how she wasn't allowed to switch from Tropical Breeze to Valentine Pink.

"She said it was your last chance if you wanted to change your room," Sandra reminds me.

"I know."

"So then why are you allowed to redo it now?"

"Because I'm special."

"That's not fair. *Mom!*" Sandra stomps down the stairs. She's such a drama queen. I didn't even say I was repainting. I haven't thought that far ahead yet.

I keep ripping stuff off my wall. I'm not throwing everything away, though. There's some stuff I want to keep, so I pull the tape away carefully from around those things. This is going to take a really long time.

A few minutes later, Mom comes in. "Sandra tells me you're ripping your room apart."

"I'm *redecorating.*"

"It would appear so."

"Why is everybody freaking out? I'm just taking some stuff down. It's not a big deal. *God.*"

"You've been sleeping a lot lately," Mom goes. "Are you feeling okay?"

"I'm just tired."

"I know the divorce isn't—"

"I don't want to talk about it."

"You have to talk about it sometime, honey. You can't just—"

"I don't want to talk about it!" I scream.

This shocks Mom into silence. I never scream.

Then she says, "What about our deal?"

Our deal was this: As long as I'm doing okay, I don't have to go back to therapy. I felt like I got everything I needed from it last year and it bothered me to keep talking about the same things. But if I'm not okay anymore, I'm supposed to go back.

"I don't need to go back," I say. "I'm fine."

I can feel it. This familiar flood of despair, like in those nightmares where you know you're going to end up falling. And I know, no matter how hard I try to fight it, that the downward spiral has me.

*

May-June

*

46

When I got to Derek's house, his mom told me that he wasn't home yet but I could wait in his room. He was supposed to be here. We had plans to go to Andrea's May Day party.

I guess he forgot. Again.

So here I am, alone in his room. A room with answers just waiting for me to find them.

The clay sculpture I made for him during the pottery unit in art is sitting on his nightstand. I pick it up and all these memories come rushing back. The first day Derek sat at my table. Asking me out when I had almost given up hoping that he liked me. Derek kissing me at Shake Shack. Taking the blurry picture of him at Cosmic Bowling. All of those intense nights, kissing him for hours.

I drop the sculpture and bend down to pick it up. There's a Rocket Dog shoe box sticking out from under his bed. I immediately want to see what's inside that box. Maybe the answers I've been looking for are right there. Or maybe I'm creating all of this drama for nothing. Maybe there's nothing serious inside. Maybe it's just a Boy Scout manual and some shells from vacations down the shore when he was eight.

But I know this story has a different ending. I know there's something going on with this box. And I know I need hard evidence so I can finally move on. I hate how jealous I am and it's making my depression worse. I can't feel better until I know the truth.

There's a chance I could get caught. Derek could come home any second and find me going through his stuff. But if he was going to be here, he'd be here by now.

I slide the box out a little and flip the lid off. There's a bunch of envelopes tied together with twine. My stomach immediately churns. This is them. The letters. From her. The ones Sierra wrote to Derek while she was away the summer they were going out. I heard that she sent him a card or a letter every single day for a month. And now here they are right in front of me and I can read them if I want to. I can read them and he would never know.

If I really want to.

If I read them, I'm just going to get upset and cry and be mad at Derek for something that happened before he even knew me. If I don't read these letters, I'm always going to wonder what they said. I'll be mad at myself for missing my chance to find out.

So I decide to risk it. I slide the first letter out from under the knot of twine. It has his name in hot-pink pen. *Hot-pink pen?* How third grade is hot-pink pen?

I only end up reading a few letters, just in case Derek suddenly comes home. They're all the same, so I doubt I'm missing much by skipping the last twenty. They're all about how Sierra misses Derek and can't wait to see him again and other assorted gooey hoo-ha.

That wasn't what I was looking for anyway. I really need to know about what's going on with them *right now*. Why didn't I think this through before? Okay, focus. Where would recent info be? Stuffed in a shoe box under your bed? Or out on your desk?

There's Derek's computer. Just sitting on his desk, sleeping. And he's still not home. And his mom is downstairs. And if Derek comes home or someone starts walking up the stairs, I could totally hear.

If Derek did what I'm about to do to me, I'd be wicked furious. But I really don't care.

I poke the mouse and the screen blinks on. Derek's e-mail is open. There's a folder labeled SIERRA. I double click it.

Half an hour later, Derek's still not home. I almost don't even care if he can tell that I was on his computer. But I make sure everything looks the same when I'm finished, just so he can't prove anything. This sucks. Not only did Derek totally forget about our plans *again*, he's still not home. Plus he's a skanky, lying manwhore.

So I leave.

The next day, Derek miraculously has time for me. He's waiting at our spot when I get to school.

"Sorry again about yesterday," he says. "I completely forgot."

I don't say anything. He should be sorry.

"It won't happen again," he insists. He also called me last night to say he was sorry. It was hours after I left his house. "So my mom said you were in my room."

"Yeah. She said I could wait for you there."

"You were in there a while, huh?"

"Well, you never came home, so yeah."

"Did you go through my stuff?"

"What stuff?"

"You know what stuff."

"Not really, no."

"The stuff in my box."

"What box?"

He sighs. "The one under my bed."

"Um, no. I didn't." I don't know where he's getting that from. I put everything back the way I found it before I left. At least, I thought I did.

Derek gives me this look like, *Yeah, right.*

"Why are you accusing me?"

"I just think you opened it."

"Okay. Let's say I opened it—hypothetically. How would you even know?"

"I remember how I put my stuff in that box. It was all rearranged."

Please. How many sloppy boys are so neat with their stuff that they know how they arranged it in a box? Five?

I go, "What are you so afraid I saw?"

Derek squints at me. "Let's just go in," he says.

I should tell him I read his e-mail. I should tell him I know. But

I can't do it. I can't admit that I know because then I would have to admit that I read his e-mail. And that's not the kind of thing good girlfriends do. Good girlfriends are understanding and supportive and they're always there when you need them.

Just like good boyfriends. Who also don't forget about your plans and keep you waiting forever. They don't lie to you about why they joined yearbook. And they definitely don't hang out with an ex who wants them back. Which is what Sierra's e-mail said. She said that she made a mistake and wants him back. It was from a month ago. Oh, and Evan's show and that after party? They totally went together. There was another e-mail planning it.

It's obvious that he wants us both. And he intends to have us both for as long as he can get away with it.

Here's the thing. Derek knows, in his heart, that he fits together better with Sierra, like pieces of a puzzle you can't deny. Which is the most depressing realization ever. Sierra broke up with Derek. That's the problem. Because when a girl dumps a boy, I don't think he ever completely gets over her. How can he? She rips his heart out, but it's still beating. And yeah, it's kind of the same for girls, but I think it's even worse for boys. There's a whole other ego thing to deal with.

Derek and me? I guess we had a connection, but he's not the One. The One would never make me feel this bad. So it doesn't matter about what kind of girlfriend I'm being. Because it has to be over. It's just like John Mayer says in "Slow Dancing in a Burning Room." When it's this bad, you have to get out or you'll get burned.

"Wait," I say.

Kids passing by sense something's up. They give us looks, walking slower than they normally would, trying to hear. I see Sterling watching us near the door. Then she looks away.

I'm like, "I know."

"You know *what*?"

"I know what's going on."

"I told you, there's nothing—"

"No, Derek." I get all up in his face, but I'm eerily calm. "I *know*."

Here's the part where he asks how I know and I have to tell him that I read his e-mail. And then he'll get mad at me and twist it around to make it look like I was the one doing something wrong. Which is true, but it's *so* not the point.

Only that's not how it goes. Derek stays quiet for a long time, staring at the grass. Something in his face changes. He knows I know. Game over.

"I'm sorry I didn't tell you," Derek says.

"Why did you keep lying to me?"

"I knew you'd freak out. I'm with *you* now. Everything's different."

"That's interesting, because it looks like some things are still the same."

"Look." Derek puts his hand on my arm. "It doesn't matter if she still likes me, okay? All that matters is what I do about it."

"Exactly," I say. "It's pretty obvious what you're doing."

"What am I doing?"

"You're flirting with her. You're spending like every day with her. You're—"

"I told you we had—"

"No!" I yell. I swear, if I hear any more of his excuses, I'm going to lose it. "Stop it. Just. Stop."

"Why are you so—"

"She wants you back. You know she wants you back. And you obviously want her back, too."

"We're not—"

"I'm done."

Derek looks relieved. "Good."

"No, Derek. I'm *done.*"

"Marisa, don't do this. I want to be with you."

"No you don't. You want to be with both of us. You want to be able to do whatever you want and have it be okay. Except, guess what? None of this is okay. And so I'm done."

I wasn't planning to break up with him. I mean, maybe under the surface, somewhere that's hard to see, I've known it had to end for a long time. I just never thought I'd be the one to end it.

47

I don't know how I got through that horrible day, with everyone knowing that Derek and I just broke up. It was all over school by third period. Not that I think he told anyone. There were enough kids around for someone to hear. And it only takes one person.

Before we broke up, I was in bad shape. But now I'm so much worse I can't wake up in the morning. I didn't even go to school today. I literally could not drag my body out of bed. It's the third time this week. If I call out from work one more time, they're probably going to fire me.

I hate that Sterling and I are still in a fight. I really need her now. But if I call her, she'll think it's just because of Derek and not because I miss her. Which, of course, I do. And Nash is super busy lately, so he can't always talk. Not that he'd want to talk about Derek. Maybe not even about us breaking up.

My mom doesn't want my dad. Derek doesn't want me. Sterling hates me now. Nash has moved on. Things fall apart, even when you think they're stronger than anything you could ever imagine.

Aunt Katie is over. I'm not sure if she came over just because she felt like it or if Mom asked her to come. Mom knows that when Aunt Katie speaks, I listen. We've been talking for an hour. I'm still in bed, in my pajamas. So Aunt Katie changed into a pair of my pajama bottoms and got into bed with me.

"We're having a daytime sleepover," she goes.

"I wish we could have one every day."

"Me too." Aunt Katie seems sad.

"Are you okay?"

She tells me about her latest date and how she really liked the guy. But then he never called her. So we're both bumming hardcore. It's an official pity party.

"It gets better," Aunt Katie says.

"Which part?"

"All of it. You'll see."

"It's hard to believe that now."

"I know. But you can't hide in bed all day."

"It's so unfair. You can be absent if you're sick, but what about if you're sad?"

"Ha! Like instead of calling out sick to work, you called out sad."

"Exactly. Why don't they have that?"

Aunt Katie pulls the blanket over her some more. "Because if people were allowed to stay home every time they were sad, no one would ever go to school. Or to work."

"All that sadness is sad."

"You're not allowed to wallow anymore. Remember what you learned in therapy—if you're having negative thoughts, switch your focus up. Try to focus on positive things."

I nod. But I can't help those thoughts. They're all I can think about.

"Derek doesn't deserve you," she says.

I scrunch over and lean against Aunt Katie. She puts her arms around me. We sit like that for a long time.

By the time she leaves, I sort of feel better. She's right. Derek doesn't deserve me. The only boy who deserves me is the one who realizes that I'm the best person he could possibly be with. Not that I know who that boy is yet. But I'll never stop waiting for him to get here.

Since I was absent today, I should probably try to catch up on homework. I am so behind at this point I don't even know what most of my teachers are talking about. Especially in geometry. It's like Mr. Wilson is speaking some foreign language and I'm the only one in the room who can't decipher it.

So I crack open my geometry book and try to figure out what page I'm supposed to be on. I keep having these nightmares about getting behind so far that the class is like four chapters ahead of the last thing I learned. It seems like my downward spiral has lasted way more than two weeks. I can't remember what it feels like to be okay.

I flip to a new page. Everything is gibberish. I have no idea what this book is talking about.

When my phone rings, I attack it. It's Dad.

"Hey, kid," he says. "How are you feeling?"

"I've been better."

"I wish I were there."

Do you? I wonder. *Wouldn't you still be here if you really wanted to be? Couldn't you have made it work out?*

Dad goes, "I hate to do this, but I have to reschedule Friday. Megan has this work party I should go to that she just told me about."

I'm so not ready to deal with Dad's girlfriend. That's what she is now. I mean, duh, anyone could see it coming from miles away, but that doesn't make it any easier now that it's real.

"Sure, Dad."

"Sorry. We'll do next Friday, okay?"

"Okay." I get that he has to go. But it doesn't make me feel any less lonely.

After we hang up, I call Nash. His cell goes straight to voice mail. I hang up without leaving a message. What would I even say to him? I wish you hadn't moved on? Where did you go?

48

The name Marisa means "sea of bitterness" and that's what I am.

Someone's knocking on my door. I don't even bother with it.

Mom goes, "Marisa? May I come in?"

I turn the page.

"I'm coming in," she says.

Stupid door that doesn't lock.

Mom comes in, looking uncomfortable but determined. She has to step over wads of crumpled paper and duck shredded posters poking out from the walls. I haven't had the energy to do anything about my room since the day I ripped it apart, so I've been living in the middle of this mess. Everything's stuck in limbo.

Then there's my violin case. For the first time ever, I notice it's covered in dust. I can't even remember the last time I practiced. I know Mr. Silverstein knows I've been slacking. Last week in orchestra, I let out a high squeak on the E string during a rest and he gave me such a harsh glare I thought he was going to bite my head off.

I pretend to keep reading.

"How are you feeling?" she says.

What a lame question. Even without the breakup or all the days I've stayed home from school, it's a lame question. She's seen me in the downward spiral before. She knows what it looks like.

She goes, "You're not talking to me?"

"I only answer questions that are worth answering," I inform her.

"I see." Mom sits in the armchair. Dad made it for me when I graduated from middle school. I love that chair. It has really wide arms made of polished maple. Dad made wide arms for me because he knew that I'd want to put drinks and books on them while I'm sitting there.

"Your school called," Mom goes. "Your math teacher? Mr. Wilson?"

I was kind of expecting Mr. Wilson to call. He kept me after class a few days ago and said I could talk to him about whatever's bothering me. I didn't know how to even begin explaining myself, so I told him maybe another time.

"What did he want?" I ask.

"He said that you haven't turned in any work all week. And that you don't participate in class anymore."

"I never participate in that class. It's *math*."

"Well, he said it seems like something's bothering you."

Mom gets up and goes over to the window. The river sparkles and flows. It looks happy in the springtime sunlight. I wish I could be happy, too.

"Marisa, if you—"

"I'm fine."

"But if you—"

"I'm *fine*." I'm not going back to therapy, which I'm sure is what she's trying to ask about again. I don't even want to hear it. I don't want to be like that ever again. I should be able to get through this by myself. I just need more time.

"You can't stay home from school anymore," Mom says.

"I know."

"And you have to do your homework."

"I know, Mom!"

"Mr. Wilson said he's willing to accept makeup work if you hand it in by Monday."

I pretend to read some more.

Mom says, "Can you put the book down, please?"

I keep pretend-reading.

"Put the book down."

I put it down.

"I'd really like to know why you're so angry at me," Mom says.

"You know why."

"No I don't. Maybe I did at first, but not anymore. I'm sorry about the divorce. I'm sorry that I had an affair. But I'm not sorry about Jack."

"Can you *not* say his name?"

Then something changes. Mom's face gets all tight. Obviously, I took it too far. Instead of just leaving the way she normally does, Mom's not going anywhere.

"Do you think I wanted things to be like this?" she yells. "Do you think this is how I wanted my life to *be*?"

I don't say anything. I don't know what she wanted.

"When is it *my* turn, Marisa? When you and your sister leave for college? I can't wait that long! Why should I have to put everything on hold?"

I have never heard Mom yell like that. I didn't know she could get that angry. That she could get that *anything*.

"I love Jack. And he loves me and we want to be together. And I'm really sorry things have to change, but that's how it is."

Mom stomps out and slams my door.

Adrenaline is shooting through me. I'm shaking and scared. I've *never* seen her even remotely close to this angry. She's completely freaking me out.

It's all too much. Breaking up with Derek because he likes someone else. Being in a fight with Sterling. Nash not having time for me anymore. Dad bailing on our plans. And now this.

Sometimes I wonder what it would be like to kill myself. Or more like, what would happen after I died. Would anyone miss me? Would they even notice I'm gone? What would people say about me?

Would being dead be better than being like this?

I'm not actually suicidal. There's a difference between really wanting to kill yourself and just thinking about it. But I can't help these thoughts. If I were going to kill myself, how would I do it? Slitting my wrists would be too obvious. Everyone does that. Pills would be the easiest way and probably the least painful, but how would I get them? And which ones would I get? I definitely wouldn't do something stupid like trying to hang myself or shoot myself in the head. Extreme plans like those could backfire and then where would I be? A living, breathing vegetable with an even worse life.

There are people in the world who are tortured every day. People are raped and murdered and live in horrible conditions and we don't even think about them. I could have been one of those people. I could be living in some war zone right now, with no running water and one leg. I should be grateful for what I have.

But somehow, knowing that stuff doesn't make me feel any better. Which makes me feel even worse.

There is a way out.

I drag my laptop over to my bed and start writing to him. I know he can help me if he wants to. I'm just not sure if he will.

How weird is it that I feel so connected to a boy I don't even know?

The whole rest of the day, I'm a nervous wreck. What if he doesn't read my e-mail? What if he doesn't realize how much I need him?

Finally, it's eleven o'clock and his show comes on.

"Okay, kids, there's someone out there who needs our help. If anyone has any advice to share, go ahead and send that in. I'm here twenty-four-seven for your listening needs."

He's going to read mine. I can feel it.

"'Hi, Dirk. I really need your advice. I was seriously depressed last year and there were days when I didn't want to be alive. Things got better for a while, but now I'm back there again. Everything sucks and I need to feel better. I listen to you every night and I know you can help me. So please help me.'"

My heart is banging out these alarmingly erratic beats and there's this scary buzzing in my ears. I hope no one can tell that the e-mail he just read was from me.

"It's from Helplessly Hoping," Dirk says. "This one isn't easy, friends. My opinion? You've hit rock bottom. Most of us have been there. But the good news is that life can only get better from here. And it will.

"I used to think that if someone hadn't been through whatever was going on with me, they could never understand, and trying to explain it to them would be useless. But it's not really like that. Your friends can always help you in some way. Even if they just listen, that helps.

"Here's an IM for Helplessly Hoping: 'Please don't hurt yourself. You'd be hurting a lot more people than just you.' And I have some hotline numbers I want to throw out there for all of you in Listening Land."

I write down the numbers Dirk says, but I'm not convinced that talking to some stranger would help. It would be like being back in therapy, except with worse advice.

"Helplessly Hoping," Dirk goes, "means you're still hoping. Which means you don't want to give up. So don't. And you're not helpless. You can fight this thing. Be strong. You were strong once and got over this; you can survive it again. And if you think you're going to hurt yourself, promise me you'll call one of those numbers.

"Man. This is one of those times when I wish I wasn't anonymous. I'm just this voice you're hearing. But who am I? I'm not an expert on any of this. I feel the same things all of you guys do. So just remember that we're all in this together. If you hurt yourself, you're hurting me and every single one of us."

That's when it all clicks for me. It really is like we're all in this together. All of us listening right now, at home in our rooms, waiting for our real lives to start. The way Dirk puts it, it's like we're all bonded in this larger way, even though we might not know one another. It's like we're part of a real family. Except this family can't be broken.

I'm not in this alone. I don't have to solve everything by myself.

When the show is over, I creep past Mom's door. I have to make things right with her soon. I really want to, but there's all this rage still in the way. If I let the rage destroy me, I'll never be the person I want to be. All Mom's really saying is that she wants to live in the Now, just like I do. Is that so wrong?

I sneak out and run across the dark grass to Nash's house. It's after midnight, so I can't knock. I pick up some pieces of gravel from his driveway and stand under his window. When I aim a piece of gravel at his window, it hits a tree and ricochets into the night. I try again. And again. This always looks so much easier in movies.

One piece of gravel finally hits his window. I wait for him to come over. His light was on when I got here, so I know he's up. I throw a bigger piece. The gravel hits his window with a resounding *crack!*

Nash pokes two slats of his blinds apart and sees me. There are lights along the dock, so he can tell it's me. He makes these frantic hand gestures that I can't read. Then he disappears. I wait.

He comes out to the yard all like, "What's going on? Are you okay?"

"I will be."

We walk out to the dock and I tell Nash everything. I tell him about my anxiety and going through therapy. I tell him how I was depressed last year and now I'm depressed again. All of these things that I've been waiting to tell someone, just waiting for the right person to hear them, everything just comes out of me. And Nash listens. He's the only person I want to tell. So I tell him everything and he's there for me, just the way I've always wanted him to be.

49

When Sterling opens her door, I know everything will be okay. She looks relieved to see me.

She goes, "Hey."

"I'm sorry," I say. "I'm so sorry."

And then she hugs me and it's this whirlwind where we're both crying and saying we're sorry and getting tissues and I'm just so happy it's over. Then we go up to her room and it's like we were never in a fight. It's like everything's back to normal.

"I really missed you," she says.

"Same here."

"It's just . . . after you started going out with Derek, I felt like I never saw you anymore. I got so tired of you bailing on me."

Of course she's right. I was a dumbass.

She's like, "But the annoying thing? Is that I could relate. I mean, not *relate*, but like if I were in your situation? I could totally see me acting the same way."

"That's no excuse, though. I shouldn't have spent so much time with him."

"No, of course you should have. But I felt really left out."

"I know. I'm sorry."

"And I felt like . . . I was happy for you, but I was also jealous. So it was this gross conflict and I didn't know how to handle it."

"That's okay."

"It just felt like you were getting this whole new life and leaving me behind."

"But you have tons of other friends!"

"You're the only one who matters," Sterling says. "I don't connect with those guys the way I connect with you. You're my best friend."

There were two things I was afraid of before I came over. One, that Sterling wouldn't want to make up with me. And two, that she'd think I came over just because I broke up with Derek. I have to make sure she gets why I'm really here.

"Just so you know," I say, "I'm not here because I broke up with Derek."

"I know. I heard . . . um, I guess I saw you guys outside that day. When you broke up?"

"Yeah." I remember Sterling standing by the door, watching us. I've always wondered what she was thinking, if she knew that was the end.

Sterling goes, "Was it . . . because of Sierra?"

"Yeah."

"That sucks."

"Seriously. But I'd rather be with someone who really wants to be with me. I mean, it sucks that we broke up, but it sucked more being together and knowing that he'd rather be with her."

"You deserve way better than him."

I know she's right. I'm just so tired of waiting. When does the waiting end and the living begin?

"I hate being lonely," I say.

"You?"

"Me what?"

"*You're* lonely."

"Yeah."

"Why would you be lonely? You have good friends and a real family."

"All that stuff doesn't matter."

"That's so weird," Sterling says. "I'd give anything to have your life."

"My life?"

"You have all these awesome things and you don't even see them. You have things I feel like I'm never going to have."

"That's how I feel about your life."

"Word?"

"Totally. You don't have to deal with the parental unit. You don't have brothers or sisters. It's just you, so you can do whatever you want."

"That's exactly why it's so lonely."

"Clarity" comes on. This is my favorite John Mayer song. It's about how it feels to wake up on the best day of your life, when all of your anxiety is gone because you're not worried about things you can't control anymore. The thing is, the song also says how that good feeling can't last. I wonder if he's right. Do good feelings always have to end?

It's awesome out today, so I go, "Let's walk on the beach."

"Perfect." We're the same way about the beach. Except instead of stones, she likes to collect sea glass.

"Here's one!" Sterling picks a transparent piece of blue sea glass out of the sand. She holds it up to the sky. Sunlight filters through, tinting her cheek blue.

It's amazing how little things can make a person so happy, when they were just feeling so sad. I'm trying to pay more attention to the little things that matter to me here in the Now. It helps to have these bits of magic to protect me when I'm depressed. Reminders that things can always get better.

I try to remember this when we go back inside. Because Sterling's talking about going to New York to meet Chris. At first I thought she was just joking because, a) he doesn't even live here so what's the point of meeting him, and b) why would she want to do something so stupid? But she's serious. At least, she sounds serious.

"It doesn't matter if Mom won't let me go," Sterling tells me from the stove. She's making pasta with pesto sauce. Emotional exhaustion always makes us hungry. "I'm going anyway."

"But what if she finds out?"

"So what? What's she going to do, ground me? She's never here."

"But what if—"

"You're giving me a headache. Just be happy for me!"

I can already tell there's no way I'm convincing Sterling to not meet Chris. She's determined to do it. And when Sterling's determined to do something, look out. Because if you're in the way, she will run you over.

"Just promise me you'll be careful," I say.

"Aw. You're worried. How cute is that?"

"I'm serious."

"Yes, it's very serious." Sterling adjusts her face to look all serious.

I watch her cook and try to think of what to say next. Except I can't think of anything, and now she's ranting about how some people don't know how to make a decent pesto.

"You can't put in parsley," she seethes. "That's like someone saying they're a vegetarian and then they go and eat fish or chicken. Since when are fish and chicken not animals?"

"Yeah, not really making the connection."

"It's just wrong, is what it is. You can't put in parsley! That's insulting!"

"So, it's just basil, or . . . ?"

"Of course not. Well, it's mainly basil and olive oil. But there are other essential ingredients. Like pine nuts and garlic."

How can I tell her not to meet Chris in a way where she won't get mad at me? No matter what I say, she'll still go. So I say, "Maybe I could go with you? You know, when you meet him?"

"Oh, yeah. Like that wouldn't look too ridiculous."

"Why?"

"You don't show up for a date with your best friend. Who does that?"

"People who put parsley in their pesto?"

"Exactly."

"And if someone was doing something crazy like putting in parsley, you would tell them, right?"

"Immediately if not sooner."

"You wouldn't just . . . like . . . know it's wrong and not do anything about it."

Sterling bangs a pot down on the stove.

"Right?" I go.

She's not answering me. She knows what I'm really asking. And she won't even dignify it with a response.

50

When Sandra sits down at the kitchen table with this weird blended drink, I completely lose my appetite.

"What *is* that?" I go.

"It's my new breakfast regimen," Sandra says in this tone like, *Duh, how can you not know that?*

"Yeah . . . what's in it?"

"Beets, carrots, spinach, echinacea . . . " Sandra takes a sip.

So that would explain the grinding noise that woke me up inhumanely early.

I pinch my lips together, repulsed. "Is it good?"

Sandra turns a page of the newspaper. This would be the newspaper that she probably picked up from our lawn at the crack of dawn, after she came home from running six miles. She's so efficient it makes me sick.

"It's okay," she tells me. "You want some?"

"I'm good." Her drink looks like mold and smells worse.

"Suit yourself," she says. Lately she's been saying things like "suit yourself" that totally don't match her age.

I go, "So . . . what's the point of your drink?"

"The *point*?"

"Yeah, like . . . why are you drinking it?"

"As opposed to what? That processed crap you're eating?"

I look down at my bowl of Frosted Flakes. As if I need more sugar. Every time I think about how much sugar I ingest every week just in my coffee, I can't figure out how my body keeps working. I started drinking coffee in an attempt to wake up from my perpetual half-asleep state and join the living. The problem is, I think I've developed an addiction.

Sandra's right again. She's right and I'm wrong.

I can't even win with cereal.

"You're going to be late," Mom warns. She's flipping through mail and pouring juice. Some juice spills on the mail.

"Do we have any paper cups?" I ask. "With like, lids?"

"What, you mean like coffee cups?" Mom says.

"Yeah, or travel mugs?"

"For what?"

"To take my coffee to school?"

Mom blots an envelope with the dish towel. "Don't you think you're drinking too much coffee?"

"Maybe. I'm not sure yet."

"I'm not working late today," she says. "Maybe we can go shopping for a new bathing suit after school?"

"Why do I need a new bathing suit now? It's only May."

"If we wait too long, the best ones will be sold out."

"I can't today," I say. "I have a ton of homework."

"How do you know?" Sandra butts in. "We haven't even gone to school yet."

"I know I'm *getting* a ton tonight. Plus, I'm making stuff up, remember?" Mom came to school last week for a meeting. It was me, Mr. Wilson, and the guidance counselor. Everyone agreed that if I make up the work I didn't do, my final grades for the semester can still be saved. My grades will obviously suck for this marking period, but at least I'll pass all my classes.

Sandra stares at me. She sips her drink.

"*What?*" I go.

"Why are you still so mad at Mom? Over half of all marriages experience separation or divorce. It's a fact of life."

Mom has a coughing fit. She tries to drink some juice.

After listening to Dirk that night, I totally understood that I need to forgive Mom. I made a pact with myself to be nicer to her, which I thought I was doing. So I'm shocked that Sandra can tell some of the rage is still there. I'm trying, it's just that I'm not there yet. Forgiving her can't be forced if it's going to mean something. It just has to happen when the time is right.

Same with getting over someone. I wish you could instantly forget about them the second you break up. But waiting for time to heal you can be the hardest thing ever. In my case, I thought it would be easier. Because when you're the one who decides to break up with someone, you're supposed to also be the one who's over them. Only, it's not like I didn't want to be with Derek anymore. It's just that all the Sierra stuff got in the way. I knew that if I didn't break up with him first, he would have eventually dumped me to be with her again.

So that's why it hurts when I see them together.

Every morning when I get to school, I try to ignore our old spot. Which is hard to do when your ex-boyfriend and his ex-girlfriend are standing in the exact same spot. Kissing in the exact same way you used to.

Seeing them like that hits me hard. I knew they'd get back together after we broke up. I just wasn't expecting it to be three seconds later. Derek is *such* a sleaze. Since he's being particularly sleazy this morning, I have to find a way to avoid their existence entirely. Maybe if I walk fast enough and watch the grass, I can zip by them without really noticing.

While I'm walking way over on the other side of the lawn, Derek notices me. And I notice him notice me. And it's too late to hide anywhere. Plus, where am I going to go? Unfortunately, I have to go inside and sit in homeroom like everything's okay. Which is not going to be possible if I look at them. Whatever I do, I should *not* look over.

So of course, I look over. And there's Derek, smiling at me.

Smiling. Like we're friends or something. Smiling while he's hugging Sierra, looking over her shoulder at me so she won't see.

He'll never change. I got out just in time.

All day, I can't wait to get home. Seeing Derek do that sparked something in me. But in a good way. Because it's time for me to get my life back. And make it better than it ever was.

I'm all fidgety and restless, and it's so hard to sit at my desk, class after endless class. I can't wait to get started. I stare at the clock for the last ten minutes of English. I have no idea what Ms. Fontaine is yammering about.

Instead of it taking half an hour to walk home, I race there in nineteen minutes. Sandra won't be home for a while. That girl has after-school activities like every single day. When I think about her schedule, I just want to lie down and take a big nap. Which is exactly what I'm *not* going to do anymore. No more naps. I want to be wide awake for everything from now on.

By the time Sandra gets home, I've finished taking down the rest of the stuff from my walls that I don't want anymore. Two stuffed garbage bags are tied by my door. I'm deciding what color to paint my walls. Sandra's going to freak when she finds out that I get to repaint, but I'm using my work money so there's nothing she can do about it. I totally lucked out that I didn't get fired after taking some days off when I couldn't drag myself out of bed. My boss is decent, so I told her the truth about why I missed some days when I called out and promised that I felt better now. She was super understanding about the whole thing.

I go down to the kitchen. Sandra's peeling an apple and reading and watching the news, all at the same time. If I do one of those things, it's a productive day.

"Hey," I go.

She doesn't look up from any of her activities.

I try again. "Can I talk to you?"

Sandra glances at me with some suspicion. "About what?" she says.

"About how I have to eat healthier. And exercise." Even though I know that exercise can make me feel good, I have a hard time believing it. The few times I've tried to do anything remotely physical I've mainly felt gross.

Up until now, I considered a walk by the river or taking the stairs to be more than enough exercise. But if I want things to change, like, *really* change, I have to make drastic changes in my life. Which Sandra is loving.

She runs up to her room and comes back down with a pad of poster paper. We sit at the kitchen table with markers and plan.

"Okay," she goes. "One, you have to stop drinking coffee."

"You mean, like, cut down, or—"

"No, I mean stop drinking it entirely. Starting now."

That. Is scary.

"And two," she says, "you have to eat more fresh produce. Fruits and vegetables are really important and you hardly eat any. It's wrecking your body and making you feel run-down."

Maybe she's right. Maybe that's part of the reason I'm always so tired.

She blathers on about my new healthy regimen and other stuff I can't eat and more things I should do. She writes everything down on the chart.

But I'm fixated on the coffee thing. I've been drinking coffee (with three or four sugars) every day for months now. So, what, I'm supposed to just . . . stop? With no warning?

"Then we have to plan your exercise schedule," Sandra says.

"My what now?"

"You have to stick to a schedule or you won't work out. I know you, remember?"

"Vaguely," I grumble.

"Do you want to run with me?"

"Run?"

"Yeah, I'm going for a run tonight."

"I can't. Nash and I are going to the drive-in."

"So let's go now."

"Now?"

"Why not?"

"Don't I have to, like, get ready? To run?"

"No, you just have to do it."

Nothing I can say will convince her that we shouldn't go running right this second. It's not raining or anything. And I did go to her for help. And if a drastic overhaul of my life doesn't start happening right away, I'll be very afraid for me. So we go up to our rooms and change and I dig out my Nikes that I only wear for gym when we have to run the mile. I hate that freaking mile.

Sandra's already stretching in the living room when I come downstairs. She explains not to hold each stretch for more than a few seconds because our muscles aren't warm yet and I could pull something. You're supposed to do the serious stretching after.

Before I know it, we're actually running. On the sidewalk. Like people who run. I feel all professional athlete about it.

After two blocks, things get worse. I have a cramp in my side and my left sneaker feels funny.

"I have a cramp," I report. "And there's something wrong with my sneaker."

"Just run through it," Sandra advises.

"How do you run through a cramp?"

"Just keep running."

"Are you trying to kill me?"

"No, I'm trying to save your life."

That shuts me up for ten more blocks.

I'm so out of breath. I feel like my lungs are going to explode. But Sandra's the same as always. She's not even breathing hard.

"How . . . long are we . . . running for?" I puff.

"I thought we'd do two miles. Until you get used to it."

"Two *miles*?" I can barely even get through one mile when we have to run it for gym. How the flippin' heck am I supposed to do two?

I can't breathe.

"Is there water?" I go.

"Did you bring any water?"

"No."

"Then I guess there's no water."

Note to self for future runs: Bring water.

By the time we get back home, I'm practically crawling. Climbing up the stairs is killing me. I collapse on my bed.

"Good job!" Sandra goes. "You want the first shower?"

"No, you go," I groan. Just the thought of dragging myself into the shower is exhausting.

But I have to get ready. Nash is picking me up soon. There's this old drive-in that they totally renovated and tonight is the opening night. Everyone who gets how cool that is will be there.

It was supposed to be me, Nash, Sterling, and Jordan, but

Sterling's sick and Jordan had a paintball tournament. I have this creepy feeling that the real reason Sterling wouldn't come is because she'd rather sit at home IMing with that online Chris guy. Which is why I wanted her to come out with us. It's obvious that Jordan likes Sterling, and maybe if she gave him a chance she could have a real relationship.

They're showing *Heathers*, which I've only seen parts of once during a Christian Slater marathon on TV. Of course Nash has seen it a zillion times. He even has lots of the lines memorized. There's nothing more annoying than watching a movie with someone who's saying the best lines along with the characters.

"Can you please shut up with that?" I go.

"What?"

"Saying all the lines."

"What's wrong with it?"

"I'm trying to hear the real lines!"

"These are the real lines. I know what I'm saying."

"Just forget it."

But five minutes later, he's all like, "No, Heather, it's *Heather's* turn!"

My annoyance isn't going away any time soon. "Can you stop?"

"I thought you said to forget it."

"Not everyone has seen this movie, you know."

"I know. Some people's lives are terribly lacking."

"Like mine right now because I *can't hear*."

"I never knew you were like this."

"Like what?"

"When did you get so bossy?"

"Just now."

After, we go to the Notch. I don't feel like bowling, though, so we decide to get blueberry crumble at Shake Shack. Birgitte is there at a rowdy table in the middle, but Tabitha's not with her. They used to be best friends, but I heard they got into a huge fight and now they're not. It makes me realize all over again how much everything has changed since last year.

"Is here good?" Nash indicates the only free table.

"Yeah, but . . . we can go somewhere else, if you want."

"I thought you wanted blueberry crumble?"

I glance over at Birgitte. I'm sure she saw us, but she's acting like she didn't.

"Oh, that," Nash goes. "No worries."

We have one of those tables that's higher than the others, with really tall chairs. These are the best seats because they're at the window and you can see everyone going by. Not like there's so much action to watch around here, but there's a good river view. Tonight, the river is dark and quiet.

My legs are killing me. At least my cramp is gone.

Nash takes the tea bag out of his mug. He didn't even admit that he liked tea until a few weeks ago. Now he drinks it in front of me all the time. He's into all these weird kinds, like rooibos, which is a red tea that's great for your immune system. Which I really should get into, since I'm off the coffee.

"No coffee?" Nash says.

"I quit."

"Since when?"

"Since five hours ago. I'm detoxing my system."

"Nice."

A boat sails across the river, painting a glossy line of lights behind it.

"So," Nash says, "are you . . . feeling better?"

"Totally. This helps a lot."

"Blueberry crumble?"

"No. Well, yeah, but . . . just being here. With you."

There's so much I want to say to him. I wish I had been feeling these things last fall, before the kiss that didn't happen, before the whole Derek debacle, before my downward spiral. There's a force pulling me toward him that wasn't there before. I'm not sure where it came from or when I first started feeling it, but it's there. Only, while I'm feeling a pull toward Nash, it seems like he's pulling away from me. Just like I pulled away from him before.

He obviously doesn't like me anymore. I had my chance and I blew it.

Nash coughs. He goes, "Yeah, so . . . I'm making summer plans. I might do this robotics camp thing. Or maybe I'll kick it in Aruba for the summer. I could use a recharge."

"Like Dirk."

"Huh?"

"Dirty Dirk. The other night he said how he wants to go to Aruba and have one of those touristy tropical drinks. You know, like in a coconut with all those mini umbrellas sticking out?"

"Oh. Guess I missed that one."

Birgitte's table cracks up in this burst of laughter. I wonder what it's like to have a big entourage like that. It reminds me of how obsessed I was before with being more social and having a lot of friends. Why was I like that? Having a bunch of friends means nothing. It's the ones who are always there for you that count. I'm lucky to have two good friends I love. That's way more special than having ten random friends.

"I need to use the bathroom," I say.

"I'll alert the media."

"Isn't that from one of your retro movies?"

"Extra blueberry crumble if you know which one."

"Nope. I'll be right back." I pass by Birgitte's table and see Sierra sitting with her. When I'm in the bathroom washing my hands, Birgitte comes in.

"Hey," she goes.

I look at her in the mirror. This could be some sort of trap.

Birgitte's like, "There's something I want to tell you."

It probably has to do with Derek and Sierra and I really don't want to hear this, whatever it is. I don't want to get dragged down into the whole drama of them getting back together.

But of course I have to know. So I'm like, "What is it?"

"I felt really bad about laughing in front of Jordan. You know . . . when he gave me that letter from Nash? I saw you watching."

Is she seriously telling me this? Seriously?

"It's just that I was nervous," she explains. "I have this laughing reaction when I'm nervous. It's so embarrassing—I always feel bad after. It wasn't because of the letter or Nash or anything."

"Don't take this the wrong way, but why are you telling me this?"

Birgitte checks her teeth in the mirror. "I know you're friends with Nash and I didn't want you to think it was anything against him. You could tell him I'm sorry. If you want."

"Well . . . thanks for telling me," I say.

"Okay. See you."

That was weird, but it gives me hope. Because it proves that people really can change, if they want to badly enough. Which means that anything is possible.

51

When Nash walks into Cosmic Bowling, at first I can't tell who it is because a shaft of sunlight is blocking my vision. Then he comes closer and I see him in this whole new way, like it's the first time I've ever seen him.

He's not Typical Nash, with a crumpled shirt and crazy hair and horn-rimmed glasses. He's got this whole new-and-improved thing going on. He's Stylin' Nash. He has a new haircut and new clothes and . . . is that *product* in his hair? He has these hot jeans that actually make him look good. He has contacts instead of his glasses. He's even, like, walking differently. Or something.

It's like he did a whole summer reinvention thing over the week-end.

"Hey," Nash goes.

I say something like, "Hauh."

"Where's Sterling?"

"Oh, she's . . . in the bathroom?" I would so rather be out on our dock, relaxing with the Nash I know. This new Nash is kind of freaking me out.

Two girls walk by and look at him. They like, *look* at him.

We get shoes and a lane, but Jordan's not here yet. So we decide to play one of the best old-school games while we're waiting for him.

"Okay," Sterling announces. "I've got one."

"I've got the best one ever," Nash counters.

"Sorry, buddy. Not as good as mine."

"Well, I guess I'll just let you go first then."

The thing about playing Most Embarrassing Moment is that everyone thinks theirs is the most embarrassing because it happened to them. They're usually too embarrassed to tell the stuff that's *really* embarrassing, so the shock value is usually on the low side. But it's still fun.

Sterling looks over at me. "Remember that time last year when I wanted to borrow your coat?"

"Not really," I tell her.

"Yeah, it was like . . . you were in orchestra and I was whispering to you from the door and you were—"

"Oh, *yeah*!"

"Do you know why I wanted to borrow your coat so bad?"

"No . . ."

"Do you remember which pants I was wearing?"

"No . . . oh!"

"Those white ones."

"Oooh."

"Yeah."

"So," Nash says, "is this, like, a female thing?"

"You could say that," Sterling goes.

"Got it. My turn. My thing is worse."

Sterling's like, "Challenge." Which means that if his really is worse than hers, he wins.

"Challenge accepted," Nash says. "I have one word for you: Birgitte."

Part of playing Most Embarrassing Moment is that you have to actually explain what you're talking about in excruciating detail. Hearing it out loud is half the embarrassment factor.

"We'll need detailed information," Sterling prompts. "Please explain."

"You're really going to make me say it?"

"That's the game," I remind him.

"Okay, okay. I liked Birgitte and I wrote her a letter and when Jordan gave it to her she laughed in my face. That's it."

"But you were down the hall," I say.

"She was laughing in my face metaphorically. It's only a technicality that Jordan's face took the fallout."

"Hmm," Sterling wonders. "Which is more embarrassing: Completely ruined white pants that the whole flippin' world can see, or liking some girl who doesn't like you back?"

"Wait," Nash goes to me. "How do you know where I was?"

"When?"

"When Jordan gave Birgitte the letter."

"Oh. I was there."

"You were *there*?"

"Yeah."

"You saw the whole thing?"

"Yeah."

"You never told me that."

"I didn't? Huh. Well, yeah, I was . . . I don't really remember, just . . . around."

Nash stares at me. "You're hiding something."

"No, I'm not."

"Yes, you are. I can always tell when you're hiding something."

"How?"

"If I tell you, will you tell me why you were there?"

"I don't need to know that much."

"Aha! So you admit that you're hiding something!"

"Do we need to be reminded of the most important rule for playing Most Embarrassing Moment?" Sterling asks. "I think we do, so here it is. You can never, under any circumstances, lie or—"

"I didn't lie!"

Sterling blocks my face with her hand. "Can I finish?"

"Fine."

"You can never, under any circumstances, lie or omit critical information."

"It's not critical."

"It's vital," Nash says.

"What's the difference?" Sterling asks. "Critical, vital, same thing."

"And thank *you*, Ms. Synonymous," I say.

Nash goes, "It's vital because she's trying so hard to cover it up. If it wasn't important, she'd have said it already."

"Said what?" Sterling goes. "How do you even know she's hiding something?"

"I can always tell," Nash says.

"You can't omit information," Sterling insists. "That's not playing the game."

I give up. "Okay, fine, you win. I'll tell you. I was there because I thought the letter was for me. Happy now?"

"Why did you think that?"

"Remember when you wanted my advice about some girl you liked? But I didn't know it was Birgitte because you didn't tell me?"

"Yeah?"

"I thought it was me. Who you liked."

"Okay . . ."

"So, I thought the letter was for me because I gave you that advice to write her something. And then I saw Jordan coming down the hall with it and I thought he was looking for me. Oh, and P.S.? Birgitte wasn't really laughing at you. She was just nervous and she laughs when she's nervous."

"You thought the letter was for you?"

"I'm pretty sure I've already mentioned that."

"But if you were the one I liked, why would I ask your advice about what to do?"

"I thought you were trying to tell me something. Like you wanted me to figure it out."

"Oh."

"Why was it so hot today?" Sterling wants to know.

We don't answer her. We're just looking at each other. Now Nash knows. And if he's smart, which he is, I'm sure he's figuring out that I wasn't completely hating the idea of that letter being for me.

"Must be global warming," Sterling proclaims.

Even though he's somewhat mellowed out, Nash still can't resist correcting someone who's crazy wrong. "Global warming isn't about one day being warmer than usual," he explains. "Or even one season being above average temperature. It's a trend that takes place over thousands of years."

"But isn't global warming a reality?"

"Yes, but not because it's warmer today. You have to consider the earth as a large-scale system, in which everything is connected."

I'm waiting for Nash to say something else about the letter incident, but he doesn't. So we all just watch the lame guy in the next lane roll a gutter ball.

Jordan finally shows up. I wait for sparks to fly between him and Sterling. But the only sparks are coming from his direction. She could not look more uninterested. And the worst part is I can tell she'd rather be here with Chris. Or at least IMing with him instead of bowling with us.

We break out into teams. It's me and Nash against Sterling and Jordan. So far, they're kicking our butts.

"You're up," Nash says.

I lift the neon orange ball I always use. Not that I bowl all that often or anything. Which is obvious by how heinous my bowling skills are. Nash is really sweet to be on a team with me. He's much better than I am.

I roll the ball. It knocks down two pins.

"You're on a tear!" Nash yells. Which is a joke, since my last roll was a gutter ball.

"I'm all about the improvement," I say.

"Obviously."

Nash gets up for his turn. Damn, he looks good. He's like a completely different person. But it's not just what he looks like that's different. His attitude is different, too. I've been noticing that he's more outgoing and he seems more relaxed around people. It's like he's the new-and-improved Nash. Nash Version 4.0.

"Hey, so, Jordan asked if I wanted to do something next weekend," Sterling whispers, even though Jordan is talking to someone playing the next lane.

"Get out!"

"I know."

"What did you say?"

"I said I was seeing someone."

"Why?"

Sterling gives me a look like, *Quit it.* I think I'm going to have to accept that nothing's going to happen with Jordan.

She goes, "Is Nash trying to get on *People*'s Sexiest Men Alive list?"

"Um . . ."

"I mean, he looks . . . *good.*"

I know he does. I was just thinking that again when Sterling said it. But I'd be embarrassed to admit it out loud. Especially since Jordan and Nash are doing this dorky dance because Nash just rolled a strike.

"He's on Marisa's team, remember?" Sterling yells at Jordan.

"Yeah, but in spirit it's girls against guys," Jordan says.

Nash comes over and sits next to me. Sterling goes up to roll.

"Nice roll, right?" he brags.

"Yeah, yeah, you rule the planet."

Nash's arm is touching mine. Is he sitting like that on purpose? Does he want me to press my arm up against his more? Or does he even know we're touching? There's that pull between us again, except it still feels like it's only going in one direction.

"Nice jeans," I say. "They're new?"

"Yeah. I just got a bunch of stuff."

"I've noticed."

Then Nash flashes me a look. And for the first time in a long time, I can see what happened between us behind his eyes. I don't know what to say. So we just stay like that for a while. Saying everything without saying anything.

His arm burns against mine.

Nash is amazing. It's like he decided who he wanted to be and then became the ultimate version of himself.

Now it's my turn.

52

Here's the good news: Sterling isn't going to New York to meet Chris.

Here's the bad news: He's coming here instead.

Which means he knows where Sterling lives. And he knows where she goes to school and he knows how to find her whenever he wants. So when Sterling realizes that he's a skeezy child molester, she won't be able to escape him.

I see a major stalking problem coming on. Sterling doesn't see anything but sparkly rainbows and puffy hearts. She was so excited when she found out that Chris is coming here I thought she would hyperventilate when she was telling me about it.

"He's coming tomorrow!" she yelled.

"Where are you guys meeting?"

"Why?"

"Just to know. In case."

"In case what?"

"In case something happens."

You could tell that Sterling was suspicious that I would show up and crash her party, but I promised I wouldn't. Of course I'm going, though. But she won't know I'm there.

"We're meeting at the park," she went.

"When?"

"Why does it matter?"

"Just so I know."

"In case something happens again?" Sterling said. But you could tell she was joking. She was flying high on a cloud of infatuation and couldn't be bothered to let anyone bring her down. "Four."

When I got to the park, I made sure that Sterling wouldn't be able to see me. I found a spot behind a tree cluster that's not too close. Sterling's sitting on the merry-go-round, waiting for some random guy she's hoping will rock her world. I check my watch. It's almost four, but Chris isn't here yet. You probably think I followed her to the park to be annoying, but actually no. I really am worried. Which is why I brought Nash with me.

"What does this guy look like?" Nash goes.

"I don't know," I say. "He's older."

"Like thirty?"

"Ew, no, he's twenty-one."

"And what are we supposed to do if he attacks her or something?"

"He won't. That's why she's meeting him in a public place."

"So why are we here again?"

"In case."

"In case what?"

"Do you want me to swat you again?"

"No, you abuser."

"In case something happens. In case she needs us."

"Fine, but I'm not into physical violence. It's not like I can kick this guy's ass or anything."

We wait. Even from all the way over here, I can tell that Sterling is getting impatient. She keeps checking her watch and crossing and recrossing her legs. It's obvious that she wants to look around, but she's trying not to. No one's approaching her anyway.

"What if he doesn't show?" Nash goes.

"Then Sterling will finally realize that meeting someone online is a stupid idea."

Some boy sits on the merry-go-round sort of close to where Sterling's sitting. She looks over at him, annoyed. Then she looks around for Chris.

"That's him," Nash says.

I don't see anyone. "Where?"

"Right there. Sitting on the merry-go-round."

"That's not him. He's way older."

"I'm telling you," Nash insists. "That's him."

I squint at the boy. I wish we had binoculars. Why didn't we bring binoculars? They always bring binoculars for stakeouts in movies.

There's something about the boy that's familiar. I feel like I've seen him before, but I can't remember where.

"That's not him," I go. "He's too young. He's like a freshman or something."

"Doesn't he go to school with us?"

Oh my god. That's it. He *does* go to school with us. He's that random freshman who plays the triangle!

I'm like, "I know him. Sort of. I mean, he's in band."

We watch him get up and approach Sterling. She looks at him like, *Do I know you?* He says something. It looks serious.

"We have to hear what they're saying," I go. "Can we get any closer?"

"Only if you want Sterling to see us." There's nothing but open grass between our tree cluster and the merry-go-round. Which means we're not going to be able to hear anything. Hearing isn't worth Sterling knowing that I was here. She'll never trust me again if she finds out.

We hear Sterling scream, *"What?"* Then triangle boy says something else. He looks desperate. She looks pissed. She gets up and stalks away. Luckily, she's not coming over this way. Triangle boy doesn't follow her.

"Why is she leaving?" I ask. "She'll miss Chris."

"Dude. I keep telling you. That *was* Chris."

"No way, that kid's name is—"

Oh. I guess my brain was refusing to believe it. Even though I suspected Chris all along, I never suspected that he'd be the random freshman who plays the triangle. That's really lame. I feel bad for Sterling, but I'm relieved that I can stop worrying now.

When I get home, I want to call Sterling to see if she's okay.

But of course I can't do that. I don't want her to know that I saw everything. So I take out my new can of paint and brushes. My walls are already painted and Aunt Katie's coming over to help me do the trim. I used her color book that has every possible color of paint in it to pick my wall and trim colors. I picked a light blue color called Zen Waterfall for the walls. It has a calming effect. And I picked a pale lavender for the trim. Aunt Katie came over a few days ago to help me paint the walls. They look awesome.

Shockingly, Sandra didn't give me the hard time I expected about getting to repaint my room. Partly it's because I used my own money to buy the paint. But I think it's also because she's my new nutritionist-slash-trainer, so we have a more professional relationship now.

After I repainted my walls, I decided not to write on them again. Or hang up a bunch of stuff in collages. I wanted to create a more peaceful space, so now my room has a very simple theme. There are only four photos on my main wall. I picked the best river photo that I took during each season, from last summer to this spring. Now they're all in identical frames, hanging on my wall in a line. Together, they tell the story of a year in my life.

I hear a car in the driveway and run downstairs. I can't wait to get the trim painted.

It's Aunt Katie, but that isn't her car. And she's not driving it. A guy is dropping her off! I didn't know she was dating anyone seriously enough to have them drop her off at her niece's house, so I can't wait to hear the sitch.

"Who's that?" I demand when I open the door.

"Don't say hi or anything."

"Hi. Who's that?"

"You didn't recognize him?"

"I couldn't really see."

"It was Campbell," Aunt Katie says like it's nothing, climbing the stairs.

"Wait. *Campbell* Campbell?"

"Do you know any others?" She puts her bag on my bed and picks up a brush. "Is this the lavender?" She points to the paint can.

"Yeah. Are you guys . . . like . . . together again?"

"We seem to be."

I'm dying to know what happened with that. I thought she didn't like Campbell anymore. What makes a person want to get back together with someone she decided she didn't want to be with?

Aunt Katie isn't talking. So we paint the trim and there's nothing but the *ffffwut-fffwut* sounds of our brushes. Which makes me miss sanding furniture with Dad. He doesn't work out back anymore. I guess it makes sense that he's totally out of the house now and all moved on with everything. It doesn't mean that he's moved on from me. Just moved on from a life that wasn't working anymore.

I'm dying to know.

"So . . . how did you guys get back together?" I ask.

"Well," Aunt Katie says, "it's complicated."

"I've got time."

She laughs. "Why are you so fascinated by this?"

"I just thought you guys were so perfect together. And you said it was the best relationship you ever had. I couldn't believe it when you broke up."

"Yeah . . ."

"So why did you?"

"I was stupid. I made a stupid decision to break up with him because I thought I could find someone better."

"But you loved him."

"I know. I don't mean better in terms of personality, but . . . better physically."

"Oh."

"How shallow can I get, right?"

Major revelation. Aunt Katie had a great relationship and she threw it all away because she was hoping she'd find a hotter guy. I guess that kind of stuff really does happen.

"I don't think you were being shallow," I say. I'm trying to choose my words carefully here. "You just . . . didn't know."

"I can't believe how stupid I was."

"I don't think it's stupid to want to be with a hottie. Isn't that what everyone wants?"

"Yeah, but then you realize that this 'whole package' everyone's looking for is unattainable. No one can be everything you want them to be."

I never thought I'd hear Aunt Katie say that. Ever since she started talking to me about her dating life, she's always been searching for the whole package. The guy who has everything she's looking for. She made a list of things he had to be: smart, funny, cute, interesting. Now she's admitting that was all just a fantasy?

"It's so hard, with dating," she says. "Everyone's always on their best behavior for the first few months, so you don't find out who they really are. You can feel like you're totally connecting and everything is all euphoric at first—that's the science of it. But after that, you're usually disappointed. That's why so many people—well, mostly women, really—are so surprised when they think they've met the person they're meant to be with and then the guy ends up leaving them."

"Wait," I go. "So you don't think the whole package exists?" Because that's exactly what I've been looking for, too. And I don't want to find out I'm looking for something that isn't out there.

"Maybe," Aunt Katie says, "but maybe the package comes in a different shape than we originally thought it would. The most important thing? Is being with someone who really cares about you."

Maybe that's it then. Maybe it's just hard to see what's right in front of you while you're frantically searching for it. And maybe I've finally found what I'm looking for.

53

Dirk is playing a song I've heard before, but I forget when I heard it or what it's called. Right before this, he was ranting about how our school just got busted for not recycling. He has a letter from some official-sounding people in the part of Connecticut where they decide what we should learn. Dirk read the letter to us, which says that if the school doesn't start recycling like it was supposed to be doing all along, it will get fined. And the story will be given to the press.

Before Dirk, we never knew how many scandalous horrors were consistently hidden from us. Don't we have a right to know what's going on with our school? Aren't we people, too?

Dirk's read so many interoffice memos and letters about teachers and students, even a ridiculously unfair letter the principal wrote about a student who was committed to a mental hospital. Dirk didn't say which student, though. He only shouts you out if you're a dumbass.

Dirk comes back on and says, "That's 'Treasure.' The Cure's intense, right? I usually listen to them when I'm bummed out. Something about the whole misery loves company thing." Then he starts reading IMs from listeners. While he's reading, I hear this dull clank that's totally familiar. He goes, "Sorry, friends. Just knocked over something I bet you'd never guess was on my desk."

Suddenly, it all clicks.

I know who Dirk is.

I go downstairs and sneak out the back door.

If this were a TV show, his room would be downstairs and I'd be able to just crawl through his window with no problem and land in his room. But since this is real life, I have to unlock the front door to get in. So when I get to his house, I look for the ceramic turtle where he hides his key. He used it one day when I came over after school and he didn't have his keys.

I'm all nervous and shaky. It being my first time breaking into a house and all. I get the door open and manage to walk quietly to his room without getting caught.

His door is closed. I put my ear against it and listen. And that's how I know I'm right.

Because he's reading IMs from listeners.

I turn the doorknob. His door doesn't lock, same as mine. I push the door open.

Nash is sitting at his desk with headphones on. His cowbell is knocked over.

He stops talking.

"Let's kick it old-school, shall we?" he says. "Here's some Dre, tellin' it like it is."

He takes his headphones off. "What are you doing here?" he says.

"I knew it was you."

"How?"

"Remember that time in lunch when you were listening to your iPod?"

"Uh . . ."

"When we were too depressed to eat?"

"Sort of . . ."

"You were listening to 'Treasure.' And you said how it makes you feel better and that misery loves company."

"You remember all that?"

"Apparently."

"So." Nash gets up. "What happens now?"

"I won't tell anyone. I promise."

"I know."

"You can just . . . keep doing the show. Everyone loves it."

"Hm." He thinks about that. "It's gotta end sometime, right?"

"Why?"

"They're trying to find out who I am. It's only a matter of time until I get busted. I never thought I'd be on for this long anyway. It's all good."

The way he brings everyone together, just by talking about real things that matter to us, is amazing. I still can't believe Dirk is actually Nash. I don't want to be the reason he quits. "Trust me, I won't tell—"

"I know you won't. That's not it."

I'm like, "How did you—"

"Find out all that stuff about school?"

"Yeah."

"I work in the office, remember?"

I totally forgot that Nash does service credit in the main office second period. He's even told me how easy it is to get information in there. He has access to all these confidential files. And the teachers and secretaries totally talk about private things right in front of him, as if he can't hear them or something.

"How did you think of this?" I ask.

"You know what?" Nash goes over to his desk and puts his headphones back on. "Let me just finish up here and then we'll talk about it. Cool?"

All I can do is nod. Dirk is Nash. Nash is Dirk.

Far out.

"Okay kids," Nash says into his computer mic. "It's time to say good-bye. And not just for the night. This is it. I won't be back. No worries: It's not you, it's me. You've all been great and I wish it could go on forever. But everything comes to an end, right?"

There's no explanation for what I'm about to do. It's like he has me under a spell or something. The pull is stronger than ever. I may be risking our friendship, but he's worth the risk.

I go over to Nash and kiss him, just the way I've been imagining.

You could totally hear that I just kissed him if you were listening. So Nash goes, "Dude. I've just been kissed by the most gorgeous girl alive. That's it for All Talk, No Action. Looks like it's all action for me!"

IMs and e-mails start flashing on his computer screen, wanting to know who the girl is. Of course, he can't tell them. Then everyone will know he's Dirk. Because I can already tell that this is the beginning of something real.

I sit on his bed and watch Nash be Dirk one last time. I still can't believe what I'm seeing.

"Last words of wisdom. If your parents are screwed up, don't turn into them. Use them as an example of who *not* to be—be yourself instead. You can overcome your fears, you can change, you can make life into what you've always wanted it to be. Maybe not tomorrow, but soon. So hang in."

A warm breeze drifts through the window, puffing the curtains out. I can hear the river rushing by. Some bells hanging near the window make delicate chiming sounds.

"Failure is not an option," Nash tells everyone. "If your life sucks now, it can only improve later. We all feel alone. We all feel desperate. Know that we're all in this together. You're not alone, no matter what. Remember that."

He puts on his last song.

"Your window's open," I say.

"I know. I keep it open all the time now."

"You do?"

"It feels so much better in here with fresh air. Don't you know that?"

The whole time the last song plays, Nash looks right at me from across the room. He never looks away.

54

They always say how eating fresh food makes you feel better, but now I know it really does make a difference. I have more energy and I feel happier. I'm not sure if that's a direct result of Sandra's nutrition regimen or just finding my way into the light after living in all of that darkness, but I'm loving it. Even my skin looks better. Plus, I gained about ten pounds when I was depressed, which I'm losing now. I'm not running with Sandra anymore, though. The one time was more than enough, thanks. I just had to accept that I cannot run. So I'm doing yogalates at Mom's gym.

The thing about having an anxiety disorder is that it will always be part of my life. But I'm not afraid to ask for help when I need it because my friends and family really care about me. They help me be strong enough to fight this.

I was supposed to be at Sterling's five minutes ago, but I'm running late. Hair emergency.

There's a knock on my door.

"I can't help you right now," I yell. I promised Sandra I'd help her with her final physical science project. It's the same exact final project I had to do when I was in physical science because Mr. Zinn assigns the same things every year. Which is why I threw out my physical science notebook at the end of eighth grade. There's no way I'm doing all the work and then letting Sandra mooch off me for a free ride.

"Maybe when I get back from Sterling's—" I yank open my door and there's Mom. "Oh. I thought you were Sandra."

"Hi there."

"Hi."

If there's one thing I learned about my time with Derek, it's that relationships are never as simple as they appear. And they're hard to maintain for a long time. Or at least, everything's constantly changing and you have to adjust to unexpected twists and turns. But one thing we all have in common is that we want to be happy. That will never change.

"Jack invited you and Sandra out to dinner tonight," Mom says. "I'd like for you to go."

I've been treating Mom better and I'm trying to get back to how it used to be between us. I never officially announced that I forgive her because I still don't know if I completely do yet. But I feel good about how things are improving with us. The thing is, doing stuff with Jack is just too much. It's weird enough that Mom has a boyfriend (who she cheated on Dad with) without having to actually spend time with him.

So I'm like, "Um, I'm going to the boardwalk with Sterling."

"Until when?"

"I don't know. Later."

"Please give him a chance, Marisa," she says. "He really wants to know you. And Sandra."

"Sandra can do what she wants."

Mom's eyes tear up. "Please."

And then she's crying. I realize that I have to accept that Jack's part of her life now, so he has to be part of mine. Whether I'm ready to deal with him or not.

I hug her. "I'm sorry," I say. "I'll go."

When I get to the boardwalk and find Sterling, I tell her everything that just happened with Mom. She goes, "It's about freaking time."

"Um, you remember what he did, right?"

"Oh, the thing where he had an affair with your mom and your parents got divorced? Yeah, I do. Do *you* remember that at least you have two parents who actually care about you, instead of an MIA dad and a mom who's never home?"

Now I feel like an ass. Sterling's the last person I should be complaining about my parents to. Actually, most kids have much worse things going on at home. I should be relatively thankful.

Sterling called me that night after she met "Chris" and told me everything. I wasn't sure she'd be okay with admitting what happened, but she told me the truth and I totally respected her for that. I also wasn't sure if she'd be mad at me for watching the whole thing. When I told her I was there, she was cool about it. I don't know how I'll ever be able to keep a straight face in full orchestra from now on. Triangle boy is too much. I mean, did he really think lying would work? Anyway, Sterling promised me that her days of online relationships are over. I made her swear to only focus on boys in real life.

"Now I have news," Sterling says.

"Hit it."

"There's a boy."

"Please tell me he's not online."

"No freaking way. He's in my new cooking class. Well, he's not technically *in* it. He helps set up and stuff."

"How old is he?"

"Seventeen."

"I'm impressed!"

"I've decided to give boys my own age a try. They can't all be rejects. I mean, look at Nash."

The breeze feels awesome. I love this time of year. I've decided to stay home this summer. Camp was great, but now there's too much going on to leave.

We walk way down on the boardwalk and I win a penguin at the ringtoss.

"For you," I say. I push the penguin at her.

"But you love these guys."

"So do you."

Eventually, they come out to meet up with us. Mom and Sandra.

And Jack.

"Hi, Sterling," Mom says.

"I like your penguin," Sandra says.

Sterling goes, "Thanks. Marisa won it for me."

Mom's like, "You remember Jack, right, Marisa?"

Here's someone I never thought I'd ever have to know, much less like. But he looks nervous, too. And if Mom likes him—no, *loves* him—then he can't be such a bad guy.

I go, "Hey, Jack."

"Hi, Marisa. And Sterling. Thanks for coming out to dinner with us."

"Can Sterling come, too?" I blurt out. I hope she doesn't kill me. I just suddenly need her there.

"Of course she can," Mom says. "Should we call your mom?"

"She's out of town," Sterling says. "And my grandma won't be over until nine."

"Then we're ready," Jack says.

So the five of us walk down the boardwalk together. It's kind of like a new extended family for Sterling, too. It's sort of awkward, but we're all trying to make things better. I can't wait to see what happens next.

55

I find him out on the dock. Somehow, I knew he'd be here.

I could already tell that the sunset was going to be incredible, so I brought my camera. I walk out to where he's sitting. He's leaning forward against the rail with his feet dangling above the water.

"Hey," I go.

Nash looks up and smiles. "Hey, you."

I sit next to him and watch the sunset begin. This summer is going to be the best. Being with Nash, swimming in the river, sharing the dock with him in this whole new way. It's kind of scary to think about how things might change. But you can't get to the place you most want to be without taking a chance. I finally found who I've been waiting for and I'm not losing him again.

We sit for a while with no one saying anything. It reminds me of that time I sat with him out here and he wasn't even talking to me. I just wanted him to know I was there.

Nash smiles at me. "This is for you." He holds out a small jewelry box.

When I take the lid off, there's a note inside. It says:

Go to the prom with me?

"You mean the junior prom?"

"Yeah."

"Why are you asking me so early?"

"So no one else does."

"I'd love to," I say.

"Yeah?"

"Totally."

"Sweet. I know you've been looking forward to it for, like, ever, so . . ."

"How do you know that?"

"Because I heard you tell Sterling."

"When?"

"Um . . . in eighth grade? I sat behind you in physical science, remember?"

Way back then, while I was talking about how my dress would look and what kind of flowers would be in my corsage, Nash was listening. I can't believe he remembers all that.

"I remember," I go, "but I can't believe you do."

"I remember everything," Nash says.

The sunset is all pink and red, burning the sky. I want to take pictures of it, and timing is everything. The colors will change in a minute and then all of this will only be a memory. But I don't pick up my camera. I want to keep this in my heart and remember it forever that way. Just like John Mayer does in "3x5." Some things just can't be experienced through a lens.

I've been thinking a lot about what happened with Derek. I think I've figured out what the problem was. We were never really friends. Not the way Nash and I are. Derek was the idea of what I wanted my boyfriend to be instead of actually being the right person for me. It's like Derek was the perfect picture, but Nash is the real experience.

"Wait," I say. "You never told me how you know when I'm hiding something."

"What?"

"Remember?"

"Oh, yeah. I *was* going to tell you."

"So tell me."

Nash lightly brushes his fingers under my eye. "You get a twitch here," he says.

"Attractive."

"Not a big twitch. Just a little twitch."

He doesn't take his fingers away from my face.

I know he wants me to finally give him a chance, to stop waiting for something I already have. Right here, under the orange sky, on the dock where we've been a million times before, everything is different.

No relationship is guaranteed to last forever. But I'm okay with being here in the Now and letting later work itself out.

So just like that, I walk out of this life. And into the one I've been waiting for.

Acknowledgments

Regina Hayes and Kendra Levin are an amazing editorial team. Your insight and brilliance have turned this book into something of which I am very proud. Working with you has been an author's dream come true. Enormous thanks to both of you for making the revision process an exciting adventure.

Claire Evans provided insightful feedback and Sam Kim designed another gorgeous cover. Special thanks to the sales and marketing teams at Viking Children's Books for supporting my books with such enthusiasm. Karen Chaplin has done an incredible job as my Puffin editor for paperback editions. And thanks to Gillian MacKenzie for making sure it's all good.

Jodi Picoult rocked my world with *The Pact*. I appreciate your warm ways and approachability. Catherine Ryan Hyde's *Pay It Forward* changed the way we see the world. Thank you so much for your amazing message of peace.

Thanks to Dr. Laila Dadvand for sharing your awareness and vast knowledge of anxiety and depression. The NYU Child Study

Center also provided information used to make this story an accurate one.

Warm fuzzies go out to everyone who works with teens and encourages kids to become lifelong readers. Teachers and librarians are made of awesome.

Ben Ruby of Barnes & Noble believed in me from the start, and for this I am immensely grateful.

Much gratitude to John Mayer for providing the answers to my burning questions. And thanks to Renee Combs for creating a super cute way for Nash to ask that question.

Pierre refuses to let me underestimate myself, and for that I thank you every day. Sparkle gluons for you. Thanks also to my friends, who are the best family a girl could hope for.

Final thanks to the energy of New York City for inspiring me every single day. There's nowhere else I'd rather be, then, now, and always.